ECHO

ECHO

Kenneth Jupp

Andre Deutsch

First published in 1980 by
Andre Deutsch Limited
105 Great Russell Street London WC1

Printed in the United States of America

ISBN 0 233 97330 3

The author is grateful to Faber and Faber, Ltd., and Harcourt
Brace Jovanovich, Inc., for permission to quote lines from "Ash-
Wednesday," "Burnt Norton," and "The Waste Land" by T.S.
Eliot.

For Frederick Vreeland

Narcissus was the golden youth of antiquity, famous for his heartless rejection of lovers whose emotional demands he was unable to meet.

In punishment for this, and in particular for his mistreatment of the nymph Echo, the gods condemned him to fall in love with his own image —

BOOK ONE

1

The story of Carol Berenson really began a year before my first visit to Los Angeles. My first and, quite probably, my last. Certainly those particular circumstances will never come together again; not now. And had I known from the start the desolation they would cause within my own life — I would have stayed away from California forever.

When I arrived people were still talking about her, wondering why Carol, of all girls in the world, should have needed to hitch a ride on Coldwater Canyon Drive at two in the morning — her father having given her a brand-new Ferrari for her eighteenth birthday only a few weeks before.

Coldwater can be an eerie road at night, winding up through hills above the expensive silence of Bel Air. Pine trees tremble, and occasionally a guard dog snarls. The moon shines, huge and orange, lighting up the woods and the great fantasy houses set back behind their electric gates.

A real-estate man named Delaney, driving home from a long evening at his mother-in-law's apartment in the Valley, saw Carol hurrying along. If he had stopped for her then, there would be no tale to tell — and he very nearly did, starting to brake as the girl turned, blinded like an animal in his headlights: a slender blonde in a white dress, with a crocodile bag over one shoulder and a silver scarf tied around her neck, brown arms raised as she called out to him.

Delaney was pulling over when he suddenly remembered an article he had read the week before in his daughter's copy of *New West* magazine — so he changed his mind, shifted his foot to the accelerator and glided on down towards Sunset.

Inside the Mustang his wife protested —

"Hey —?"

"You want to stop?"

"Well, for God's sake —"

"You want to stop and get mugged, is that right?"

"By a girl —?"

"No, by her boyfriend, who's waiting in the bushes! Don't you ever read? They use girls now — it's a whole new thing."

"She looked scared to death!"

"They teach them how to do that," said Delaney tiredly, shifting the selector lever. "California's a jungle, baby."

Mrs. Delaney sighed, but did not contest this statement. She turned and stared back at the pale, diminishing figure by the roadside.

Carol was standing there, trying to comprehend that this could happen to her — that she could be passed by. She drew several deep breaths, the way they had taught her in yoga class, fumbled in her bag for cigarettes, tipped one out, lit it with shaking hands and blew a cloud of smoke towards the sky. She put the lighter away and removed her shoes, which were too tight. She pushed them into her bag.

Then, face set and determined, she trudged off barefoot down the long, silent canyon.

2

When the Toyota appeared, chugging uphill towards the Valley, Carol ran out straight in front of it. She had to jump aside to avoid being knocked over. The truck rattled on without a pause, and Carol had turned downhill again — almost weeping with frustration — when she heard the creaking of brakes. She turned. Miraculously, it had stopped. A flapping tarpaulin covered the open rear end and, as she ran back, it moved aside to reveal an owl-faced man. He gazed after Carol, then peered around cautiously at the thickly wooded countryside. Moonlight gleamed on his steel-framed spectacles.

Carol looked up at the driver — a thin-faced man wearing a military-style peaked cap and (although Carol could not see it) holding a U.S. Army revolver under the seat.

"Late to be hitching, lady."

"I'm not hitching, I've just been left here! Can you get me to a telephone?"

He glanced at his second passenger — a dark man with a hook-nose. Both wore rough workman's clothes: denim overalls, leather jackets. The passenger shrugged. The driver nodded.

Carol ran around to the passenger side. The hook-nosed man descended, holding an ancient guitar. She smiled gratefully at him and climbed in. He closed the heavy door, hitched up his trousers, and walked to the back of the truck.

Carol sank into the passenger seat.

"Thank God!" she said. "I've been a real idiot tonight."

The driver watched as she opened her expensive bag with the golden *C* embossed upon it and took out a packet of Virginia Slims. He thought she was the prettiest girl he had ever seen. She reminded him of Miss California, the year they had pinned her up in the john, whenever that had been. The year E Company had been assigned to Task Force Barker, and they had all moved into the Quang Ngai area.

He accepted a cigarette, noticing the signet ring and the gold wristwatch. Definitely good news. Carol lit the two cigarettes with a Dunhill lighter; her hands were shaking and he had to steady her wrist.

"So you got left, huh?"

"Can you believe it? By a man who just took off. In my own car, too."

The driver glanced into the back of the truck, past a pile of second-hand hi-fi equipment; the hook-nosed man had settled down, guitar on lap. The spectacled man watched in reverential silence as he began to pluck a few chords. The driver revved the engine and engaged first gear.

"You must've upset him, lady."

The truck lurched onwards, tarpaulin flapping. Carol sank deeper into the passenger seat. She looked at the electronic equipment; the revolver; a pile of *Melody Maker* magazines on the floor; a second guitar.

"Are you in the music business?"

"No, we're in the removals business."

He revved the noisy, worn-out engine again and engaged a higher gear.

"So what did you do? To upset your friend?"

"Nothing, believe me." She laughed briefly. "Not a thing."

The driver concentrated on a sharp bend.

"Maybe that was it."

She studied him as the moonlight cut across his thin face. He seemed to be smiling, as far as she could tell. Then he straightened the wheel and continued, conversationally. "I mean, maybe you should've blown him or something? He might've stuck around then."

Carol did not reply. She concentrated on the road ahead as it wound upwards through the densely wooded countryside and reflected that this was certainly not her night. However, there were pinpoints of light in the distance, hardly bigger than the stars: it would not be long now.

3

"Is that Ventura ahead?"

The driver did not answer. He appeared to be looking for something off to the right.

"Listen, uh —" Carol leaned forwards for emphasis. "If that's Ventura, there's an all-night gas station on the Freeway. I can call my father from there."

He did not seem to hear. The truck was slowing down.

"Did you go to a party tonight?" he asked absently, still looking off to the right.

"Yes —"

"Do you like parties?"

"Why are we stopping?"

As the canyon reached its highest point on Mulholland, the Toyota came to a halt — then veered sharply right past Hidden Valley Road. It bumped a hundred yards along a dirt track through close groves of mingled palms, olives and eucalyptus. Carol tried to stay calm.

"Where are we going?"

"To your next social engagement."

He braked to a halt, switched off the engine, removed his peaked cap and threw it behind him. He sighed deeply, and ran his fingers through his short, wiry hair. He stared up through the windshield at the high, moonlit trees. A night bird cried sharply and it reminded him of the sound the gooks had made that time they had been rounded up in the rice paddies, after the hamlet had been cleared and E Company was headed back to refuel. When C Company brought in another fifty villagers and forced them to squat in a circle, he had wondered why the hell they had taken so many useless prisoners — but he soon found out.

Carol tried to keep her voice steady.

"This is a bad idea —" she began.

"I think it's terrific," he replied.

Carol sat still, estimating the odds. She looked at the revolver and wondered if she could grab it before he did. How fast could she turn and open the door? How easily could he catch her if she did? A bump in the rear of the truck made her turn: the other two men were getting out. Carol decided that reason was her only hope.

"Listen," she said. "I'd better tell you who I am."

"It doesn't make too much difference, lady."

"I'm J.P. Berenson's daughter."

She waited for this information to have its usual galvanizing effect; and indeed he did look at her for a moment, raising thick eyebrows.

"No kidding."

"Yes really, and listen —" She leaned forwards again, speaking eagerly, confidentially, trying to humor him, to make an ally of this gaunt-faced horror. "He'll be real grateful if you take me home. He once gave someone five thousand dollars just for finding my cat!"

"Your cat?"

"And what I'll do, I'll say you saved my life. And who knows, maybe you did? I mean, if you hadn't stopped? So he'll give you anything you want, I promise."

That was when the driver hit her for the first time, experimentally, with the back of his hand across her face. Carol reeled away and fell against the passenger door, clutching her cheek. She stared at him, horrified; then she twisted sharply and struggled to get out. He watched in silence as she pushed and shoved at the door, finally tumbling from the truck — straight into the arms of the hook-nosed man.

[9]

She fought furiously then, kicking and scratching and trying to knee him — but he held her easily as a doll while the driver descended and strolled around the truck, the Virginia Slim still in his mouth. He stood in front of Carol and blew a cloud of smoke into her face. Then he hit her again, much harder this time, with the back of his other hand — the one with the turquoise ring on it. She gasped, and began to whimper.

"Let her go," said the driver.

The hook-nosed man stepped back, and Carol sank to her knees — then scrambled up again, still clutching her crocodile bag. She turned to run but the spectacled man appeared from the rear of the Toyota and stood there smiling — and blocking the only path of escape.

Carol paused, trembling in the middle of these well-drilled maneuvers. Blood was seeping from the gash in her left cheek. The driver removed his leather jacket and tossed it across the hood of the truck.

Everyone waited.

Carol took a step sideways towards the spectacled and (for some reason) least frightening man, and cried out — "Help me!"

No one answered, but the hills above Bel Air play tricks with sounds — and from the depths of the canyon came the suggestion of an echo:

"Help me!"

The spectacled man just went on smiling, so Carol turned back to the driver. She was beginning to gabble now: "Look, you can take my bag, it cost a lot and so did my lighter — the lighter's gold —"

The driver accepted the proffered bag and threw it onto the ground. Carol backed away, trying to unfasten her wristwatch.

"My watch is from Cartier, you can have that too —"

She stopped backing when she stumbled against the hook-

[10]

nosed man. The driver moved towards her. He reached out and ripped away her silver Hermès scarf — and most of the top of her dress with it. Carol staggered, almost fainting.

"We've got a real smart-ass here," said the driver.

The hook-nosed man chuckled.

"J.P. Berenson's daughter, no less."

"No kidding?"

"Hitching at night, like most heiresses."

He hit Carol again. She spun with the blow and then, summoning her last reserves of courage and outrage, made her dash. She was quick but the hook-nosed man was quicker, catching her wrist and twisting her arm behind her so that she fell back against him in the deep moon-shadow of the truck.

When the driver moved in front of her Carol began to scream, and the hook-nosed man clamped a huge hand over her mouth; she bit into it violently; he grunted with pain and punched her in the back of the neck so fiercely that she almost passed out. The driver gathered up the silver scarf and then, slamming Carol against the hood of the truck, bound her wrists with it. The hook-nosed man rummaged under the passenger seat and produced an oily rag, which he rolled into a tight ball; then — pinching her nose between thumb and forefinger until she gasped for air — he rammed it into her mouth.

After that they hauled her off the hood, propped her against a charred oak tree, hoisted her up and attached her wrists to a thick branch above her head. The spectacled man was still smiling as Carol swayed there, her feet just clearing the ground; when she began to jerk and twist he rubbed his head in a puzzled way and sat down on the ground.

The light dimmed for a moment as a cloud crossed the moon; muffled, meaningless sounds came from the struggling shape. There was the far-off drone of cars on Ventura, and somewhere a dog barked, incessantly.

[11]

The hook-nosed man cleared his throat as the driver removed his wide, metal-edged belt.

When he began to flog the girl, the spectacled man looked away.

4

The morning sun rose marvellously above the ash-blue hills, accompanied by a sea of insect noise.

The spectacled man was sitting cross-legged on the ground, his head resting on his arms. He raised his face to this golden dawn, then put on his spectacles and watched the dry trees gain color in the first light. Beyond him, sprawled among blankets on the ground, were the driver and the hook-nosed man, untidily asleep.

Carol was lying at the base of the charred oak — a mangled heap. Her white dress had been torn to shreds and strewn around the shrubbery.

The spectacled man shook his head disapprovingly. He stood up, went to the truck and urinated against the back wheel. To the sound of birdsong he folded back the tarpaulin, poured water from a plastic bottle into a metal kettle, set it upon a gas burner, and applied a match. Then he pulled a large canvas duffel bag from beneath the stereo equipment and, while the water boiled, he wandered around, meticulously tidying up what remained of the white clothing and pushing it into the duffel bag.

Carol was lying face downwards, her head at an awkward angle; her hands were now tied behind her back by the scarf, and the visible side of her face was cut and swollen. The spectacled man touched her lacerated arms and noticed that she still wore the Cartier watch; he removed this, and pocketed it. Then, reaching under her face, he gingerly took hold of one end of the oily rag and withdrew it from her mouth.

Next, firmly gripping her ankles, he bent the legs back until her feet were close to her hands and deftly tied all four together with the scarf — thus wrenching her body into the smallest possible shape. Holding the duffel bag open with one hand, he tipped her into it with the other — thereby tidying her away too.

He looked around the now orderly clearing, and nodded with satisfaction. He picked up Carol's crocodile bag, poured the contents out onto the ground, and considered them carefully. He pocketed the gold lighter and a fat black pen. Then he studied her California driver's license with considerable interest, unscrewed the pen and inscribed something across the face of it.

At that moment the metal kettle began to whistle loudly and his companions stirred. The spectacled man gave Carol's crocodile bag a methodical wipe with his sleeve and shoved it into the duffel bag after her. He stood up, hurried over to the truck and lifted the kettle from the gas burner. He transferred several spoonfuls of coffee from a glass jar to an enamel pot, poured in the boiling water, set down the kettle.

Then with a bright smile of greeting he turned towards the two rapists as — coughing, scratching and yawning — they rose to greet the day.

5

The time was still only six-thirty A.M. when the truck turned back onto Coldwater Canyon Drive. As it resumed its journey towards the Valley, the tarpaulin was raised and the duffel bag thrown out; it hit the road with a heavy thud and rolled a few feet before coming to rest. Carol's driver's license had been pinned to the bag. Across it had been printed the legend RENDER UNTO CAESAR THE THINGS WHICH ARE CAESAR'S.

Before the sun shadows had moved six inches across the road, police sirens were whooping and flashing, and black-and-white squad cars were screaming up the canyon. The first, containing Superintendent Larry Kellerman from the Robbery-Homicide Division of the Los Angeles Police Department, swerved around the final bend and braked to a halt beside the group of motorists gathered there.

A California highway patrolman saluted Kellerman, and led him through the crowd to the duffel bag, which was being guarded by a second patrolman. Their huge motorcycles were parked nearby. Simultaneously, ambulance unit B-1 arrived, followed by two backup units and a fifth car containing LAPD photographers and fingerprint men. Altogether some thirty people stood in silence as Kellerman squatted down, lifted the top of the duffel bag and looked inside. A few strands of blonde hair tumbled out onto the road.

Kellerman stood up. The police photographer snapped some quick shots before the fingerprint men slid a plastic cover over the duffel bag and the ambulance men carried it away.

The photographer turned to Kellerman.

"Who gets to tell her father?" he asked.

Kellerman sighed deeply.

The patrolmen waved on the Sunday motorists, and the ambulance took off downhill to L.A.

6

John Paul Berenson sat in the back of a chauffeur-driven Rolls-Royce. His hands were clenched, and his expression was like stone.

He did not at all resemble a millionaire. If you saw him anywhere outside of his cars or his houses you would never have dreamed that he was one of the richest men in America. More than anything, he looked like a University professor. He bore a strong resemblance to the late Robert Lowell; and even if you only saw him walking down a street, or into a restaurant (highly unlikely as he rarely did either) you would definitely have put him down as a poet, or a scholar of some sort.

Only his eyes were memorable. They were dark and eloquent and you saw them from across the room. At one moment alive with warmth and humor, they could suddenly snap, as through some trick of the light, and freeze you in your tracks. They were remarkable eyes: the kind for which an actor would trade in the rest of his equipment.

At that moment, as he sat in the back of the air-conditioned Rolls, J.P. was struggling for calm: and the effort had brought out a thin line of sweat along his upper lip. The superintendent's news had struck at the core of his being. Kellerman had known this, of course, and feared the call accordingly; for almost the only generally known fact about Berenson was that — since the death of his wife in 1969 — he had devoted his life exclusively to his daughter. No one knew exactly why this should be, but no one had any doubts about it, either.

J.P. unclenched his hands and ran a finger along his upper lip. Then he stared past his chauffeur towards the two highway patrolmen who — sirens blaring — were shepherding traffic aside, jumping stoplights and carving the fastest path to the Cedars-Sinai Medical Center.

Simultaneously, Carol was being wheeled down a hospital corridor; her body was untied now, and she lay twisted and contorted on the trolley; she was partially covered by a white sheet, and accompanied by a flock of hurrying nurses and doctors.

The Rolls turned through the hospital gates and braked at the main entrance. J.P. was out before it stopped, vaulting the steps three at a time. His barrel-chested chauffeur descended and spoke to the highway patrolmen, who nodded, reversed their bikes, and roared away.

A shining hypodermic needle slid out of Carol's arm. A doctor looked down. She was still unconscious. Her legs and back had been straightened out, but her face was terribly disfigured. The doctor moved aside as the door opened and Berenson came in.

And saw Carol.

He caught his breath, hunched his shoulders.

There was a pause.

"She's going to live," said the doctor.

A squad car pulled up beside the Rolls. Kellerman got out, feeling that he had aged a couple of years that morning. He left two officers in the car and hurried up the steps.

A nurse stopped him outside Carol's room.

"Her father's with her."

Kellerman nodded, and prepared to wait.

Inside the room, J.P. had scarcely moved. He just stood there, gazing down at Carol. When the nurse entered, he did not turn. She spoke to the doctor, and the doctor spoke to him, but he did not hear. The doctor had to repeat it: "The Superintendent's here."

7

The doctor's office was a plain white room with leather furniture and a rather bad painting over the desk of horses by the seashore. Kellerman was staring at the painting and rehearsing his speech; but when the door opened and they came in the speech went out of his head, because he had never seen Berenson look like that before.

The doctor sat down at the desk. J.P. crossed to the window and stood, studying the traffic on the palm-lined boulevard below.

At last he spoke:

"Render unto Caesar the things which are Caesar's."

"They knew who you were from the license," suggested Kellerman.

"Or from Carol."

Kellerman stared at him.

"She had some strange friends," said J.P.

It hurt him to say this, but he was not a man to shirk issues. When the superintendent began to protest, he interrupted: "How else did they get her, Kellerman? How do you stop someone like Carol in a fast car at night?"

"She could've broken down —"

"In a new Ferrari?"

"She could've gotten a flat, or run out of gas —"

J.P. turned back to the window.

There was a silence.

"Or —" Kellerman was improvising, "she could've switched cars at some earlier point in the evening. Three possibilities.

Either way the Ferrari is our lead. With the girl in Salinas, we had nothing."

"You still have nothing," said the doctor.

"We have sketches. OK, they're vague. She was hitching at night with no moon, plus she was stoned. Carol must've seen them better."

"You're sure they're the same men?" asked J.P.

"The same injuries. The same bruising and belt marks. The same type duffel bag and the Biblical quote — 'Thy will be done,' in her case."

"And you're sure there are three of them?"

"Minimum."

"How do you know that?"

Kellerman looked at the doctor.

"There were three grades of sperm," said the doctor.

J.P. closed his eyes. His face was pale.

Kellerman decided this was the moment for his speech:

"My guess is they're ex-service. The duffel bags are Vietnam-issue, and the belt marks are — consistent. The Salinas girl described one man as dark, with a hook-nose. Another wears steel-framed glasses, army-style. And the third is a thin-faced guy in a peaked cap. They drive around in a beat-up truck."

Kellerman paused, rubbing his eyes. The doctor concluded for him: "Of which there are thousands in California. Not to mention veterans, with or without glasses."

"So what have you done?" asked Berenson.

"I've taken charge myself," said Kellerman. "As of today everyone's reassigned. We're running a check on all state military institutions for discharged junkies, shell-shocks and religious nuts. Plus every truck theft on record."

"Were there any prints?"

"All wiped. But we're checking every house on Coldwater, plus every inch of that canyon. There'll be decoy hitchhikers on the roads tonight, and there's an all-states on the Ferrari."

J.P. turned back to the window and looked down at the boulevard.

The two highway patrolmen were returning, a white Porsche between them.

"My daughter went to a party last night, with Howard Vance. I've asked him to join us."

There was a tap on the office door. The doctor called "Come in" and Kellerman's driver entered, notebook in hand.

"Radio message." He read it out. " 'Victim Berenson reported seen two a.m. Coldwater Canyon on foot, alone, apparently hitching. Witness drove on by. Wanted to stop but wife feared could be a setup.' "

"Thanks, Jerry."

The officer nodded, glanced curiously at J.P., and went out.

There was a silence.

"So that's how they got her," said Kellerman.

8

Howard Vance sat on the leather couch in the doctor's office, crumpling and recrumpling a copy of the *L.A. Times*. He wore tennis clothes and had already said "Jesus" several times.

Howard was the kind of man people found it difficult to like; but to be honest most of that was due to jealousy. He was almost a caricature of the one-who-gets-the-girl-in-the-end: dauntingly fit, tanned, dieted, exercised; a physical presence with masses of black hair who had twice been mistaken at film premieres for Burt Reynolds (the twin pinnacles of his life, according to his friends). He had been disturbed at his morning workout and even now, in the air-conditioned hospital, he was sweating — heavy thighs sticking noisily to the leather.

"Tell us about it, Mr. Vance," said Kellerman.

"What can I say? She left around midnight."

"Alone?"

"Alone."

"And you stayed on?"

"Until three, four o'clock."

"Did you personally see her leave?"

"Sure. I was taking shots on the beach and I saw the Ferrari reverse in the drive, and then off."

"And you let her go, Howard?" asked Berenson quietly.

"What could I do, John? I was working — you know that!"

"Who took her to the concert?" asked Kellerman.

"A whole crowd — I got the seats but I was filming the

show so I fixed for her to go with Sally and Bob and that actor, what's his name, from 'Streets of San Francisco'."

"Then you all went to the party?"

"Sure. Everyone. The whole music scene. The guest list's right there."

He threw down Sunday's *L.A. Times.*

"Whose party was it?" inquired the doctor.

"Milton Rubin's. He has the old Fairbanks place at Malibu now. Spent nearly as much on the party as he did on the concert — catered dinner for two hundred —"

"And Carol left early?"

"I don't know why. I didn't see her much. My deal with Milton was to take pictures, and when you have that many celebrities under one —"

"How did she seem?" interrupted Kellerman.

"What?"

"Happy? Excited?"

"Terrific, at the concert — best rock she'd ever heard! I have her on film, going crazy in the front row. Then she was kind of speedy at the party, looking great and — bubbly, you know?"

"She had a date, Howard," said J.P.

"I guess so."

Howard paused.

"But what could I do?" He suddenly seemed quite bereft. "I couldn't have stopped her anyhow."

J.P. turned away.

Howard gathered himself. "But listen, we're talking as if Carol's dead! I mean, she's going to tell us about it, isn't she?"

The telephone rang. The doctor answered. He listened for a moment, then held the receiver out to Kellerman.

"It's for you," he said. "They've found the Ferrari."

9

The yellow sports car had been driven off the Coast Highway, and very nearly straight into the Pacific, at Malibu.

It had crashed through a private driveway, crumpling its right front fender against the gatepost, swerved alongside the house and onto the beach at the back before stopping, presumably just in time, at the very edge of the ocean. The car now stood, wheels half submerged in the sand, water lapping against the bumper. It was surrounded by policemen, who had sealed off the area.

When Kellerman walked onto the beach, accompanied by Howard and Berenson, the photographers were again at work. Two sergeants from the Scientific Investigation Division of the LAPD were dusting for fingerprints, while a forensic chemist was checking the car for blood and hair. The day's temperature had climbed into the nineties. Crowds of Sunday sightseers, oiled and bikinied, had swarmed up from the public beaches in Santa Monica. Word had gone out that this was Carol's car, and a highway patrolman had already radioed the L.A. Sheriff's Office for backup units to control the crowd and the traffic.

Kellerman looked inside the car and said something to a fingerprint man, who nodded and twisted the ignition key. The powerful motor roared briefly, and was then switched off. Kellerman returned to J.P.

"There's a half tank of gas, and no sign of a breakdown. Plus the stereo's there, and a box of tapes, so it was no robbery either. Whoever emptied Carol's bag would have stripped the car." Kellerman followed the thought. "So, someone else drove her to Coldwater."

J.P. gazed at the silent, shuttered windows of the beach-house.

"Who lives here?"

"A man called Kosinski. He's a record producer and he's been in South Africa for three months." Kellerman pointed along the white strip of sand. "Rubin's place is there. Six down."

J.P. nodded and looked up towards the gray, crumbling cliffs of Malibu. Two LAPD helicopters were circling above.

"But why is her car on the fucking beach?" demanded Howard.

No one seemed to have an answer for that; Howard went on staring at the Ferrari, then turned impulsively to J.P. "I asked her to marry me the day you gave her that car!"

"I know, Howard."

"Jesus, she was so happy."

J.P. did not reply. He stared out at the creamy blue of the Pacific.

Howard shook his head, glanced again at the somber group of men around the Ferrari, and had a sudden flash of Carol laughing, spinning the wheel, wide tires singing over gravel in the courtyard at Avonhurst. The top was down, and her blonde hair was tied back and she brandished her first driver's license in triumph as Howard parked his Porsche, jumped out, grabbed a camera and stood there, clicking away, turning around on his high-heeled cowboy boots. She swerved right up against him and he leaned across the hood getting a close-up and she was still laughing when she jumped up barefoot onto the maroon-colored passenger seat, arms raised to the sky.

"What luxury!" she cried, while he went on snapping everything, Carol, the car, the interior —

[25]

Then she slid down, tipping a lever so that the seat back sank away to the horizontal and she grinned up at him from the deep leather depths.

"I just can't wait to make it in this car," she said.

10

Now she lay propped up on white pillows, hands folded in front of her, gazing at a TV screen.

Her eyes were moving fractionally, the pupils dilating to accommodate the screen images, but her expression was blank. The cuts were healing, the bruises had paled, but the disfigurement looked permanent. Her face had somehow been jolted out of synch.

Berenson entered the hospital room and smiled at her, but her eyes did not rise from the screen. His smile faded and he sat beside the bed. He stared hard at her for a moment, then put his face in his hands. The air reverberated with dialogue from "Gunsmoke."

Berenson pulled himself together, reached out and switched off the TV. The change in Carol was instant: as the image died her eyes widened, her mouth gaped, her hands twisted into the sheet; she began to sweat; she turned imploringly to her father and a terrible whimpering began, deep in her throat; as her agitation grew she tried to tear off the bed-clothes, to sit up; she was gasping for air —

J.P. switched the set on again.

The sound spluttered back, the image returned and, as Carol relaxed, sinking down into the pillows, the whimpering ceased.

Berenson took a handkerchief from his pocket and carefully wiped the perspiration from her face.

She looked at him while he did this and it was only then he saw that her sweat was mixed with tears.

11

"It is a not uncommon effect," the neurologist was saying. "Speech loss after such a trauma."

He was standing on a balcony at the hospital — an immensely distinguished-looking Swiss-German, radiating assurance.

"Hence your English expression 'struck dumb with fear.'"

"But for how long?" asked J.P.

"In this area, who can say? I have known cases of permanent disability — but those were older patients. Carol is young, organically sound. Everything works, the vocal cords, the larynx. She will speak again. In a week, in a month —" He paused and shrugged. "The effects of shock are unpredictable. I have in Zurich a patient all of whose hair fell out — every hair of her body. Another, a young French boy, who is apparently blind. He witnessed an event of such horror that his brain now rejects the evidence of his eyes. A third who cannot move — paralyzed by fear! But they are all young, and will recover as the traumas fade, as the images of shock diminish."

"And if not?"

The neurologist hesitated.

"If after, say, one year there was no improvement, we might consider other courses. But they will not be necessary. Take your daughter home, sir. Give her calm and quiet in her own surroundings. There must be no excitement. Only peace."

J.P. looked at him.

"What other courses?"

"Do not concern yourself."

"Shock therapy?"

"This is to be avoided at all cost." The doctor spoke with feeling. "Only for truly hopeless cases — for patients with whom the image of the trauma shows no recession, but rather remains constant or even grows. At such times we might risk to reconfront the patient with his fear, in the hope that his conscious mind may now revalue and perhaps reject it. But what a perilous course! It can go either way, you see? Sometimes we merely redouble the terror, and find a madman stands before us."

"Instead of a vegetable?"

The doctor sighed. "You wish to consider the worst, of course. All intelligent men do this. But your daughter will recover, believe me. She needs only time and rest — and a permanent trained nurse."

They turned back into the room.

"And this TV obsession?"

"It will pass."

"She doesn't even know what she is seeing —"

"She knows, but does not care." The neurologist was reassuring again. "The movement and the color soothe her, as with a child."

"An eighteen-year-old child."

"So, we meet again next month? Either here, or in Zurich."

He clapped a friendly hand on J.P.'s shoulder as they crossed to the door.

"And do not worry for the TV. After all, it tranquillizes half the human race — why not Carol?"

12

A small crowd, mostly journalists, police and photographers, waited by the hospital gates on the dull, foggy morning of Carol's discharge.

Kellerman's squad car was parked in the forecourt between Berenson's Rolls and a yellow Pacer. Two highway patrolmen stood nearby.

When Carol appeared at the top of the steps, J.P.'s chauffeur leaped out and opened the rear door. She descended carefully, escorted by Howard Vance and a uniformed nurse. Her Garboesque outfit had been selected for maximum concealment: loose cotton dress, dark glasses, wide floppy hat. She had almost reached the Rolls when a photographer slipped past the police on one gate, ran across the forecourt, snapped six shots, and disappeared through the second gate. No one followed him.

J.P. watched from the top of the steps as Carol was settled into the car. Kellerman joined him.

"I'll be in touch."

"I hope so, Kellerman."

Something in J.P.'s tone made the superintendent bristle. "I've already tied up half the department! We've conducted four hundred interviews to date, plus we've —"

"I knew you're working." J.P. interrupted. "You wouldn't want to end your career on a down note."

"That's not the reason, Mr. Berenson."

"But you are due to retire soon?"

Kellerman sighed. "We don't know each other too well, do

we sir? But your father and I were close. I was just a young cop when I was first able to help him —"

"When you were first able to keep quiet, Kellerman?"

The superintendent — who had not imagined that J.P. could know this — did not reply.

"Carol is his only grandchild."

"You don't have to tell me." Kellerman produced a plastic envelope and handed it to J.P. "This was in the Ferrari."

J.P. opened the envelope and looked at the white powder; he was about to pocket it, when Kellerman intercepted the move —

"I'll keep that."

Berenson paused. "You owe a debt, superintendent."

"I know."

Berenson studied him for a moment, shrugged, then surrendered the envelope. The two men walked down the hospital steps.

"I'll have to question her friends," said Kellerman.

"What friends?"

"Her boyfriends. The ones she dated —"

"Carol is engaged to Howard Vance."

"Isn't that kind of a loose arrangement?"

"It's a family arrangement."

"But if we can only find out who drove her there — you said yourself she knew some weird people —"

"Leave it. Carol was alone when your veterans got her. Find them — that's your business. Her private life is mine."

He joined his daughter in the back of the Rolls. The chauffeur closed the door, then climbed into the driver's seat, next to Howard. The nurse waited at the wheel of her Pacer, revving the engine.

Kellerman sighed again and watched the Berenson car swing past a line of police and out through the gate of the hospital. The highway patrolmen kick-started their bikes and roared off in escort formation.

[31]

Outside the hospital, photographers danced backwards, colliding with each other as they clicked away at the Rolls.

For a moment Carol's face appeared in profile on the car window, then she was gone.

13

The fog was beginning to lift on Benedict
as the road twisted sharply and the chauffeur leaned slightly
to his right.

They were climbing high above Beverly Hills and Berenson
was sitting forwards, elbows on his knees. Carol still gazed
silently out of her window. Howard swivelled around, one
arm along the back of the seat.

"She looks better, huh?" His heartiness sounded terribly
false.

J.P. did not seem to hear; he murmured "Carol?" and she
turned towards him. She sat quite still as, with infinite care,
he removed her wide-brimmed hat and then adjusted her
hair — straightening it and fluffing it out a little from her
face. She allowed him to do this, but her expression remained
totally blank. When he had finished she turned away and
resumed her contemplation of the passing canyon.

"The neurologist was pleased, huh?" asked Howard.

Berenson did not reply. He was remembering a high-school
sports day two years before when Carol had won some swimming race or other, he forgot which, and they had presented
her with her prize in the sunshine, to much cheering and
applause, and her hair was still wet and sticking to her head
when she had run to him still in her bathing suit and carrying
the silver cup and he had kissed her and hugged her until
he was soaked himself and he had been fluffing out her hair
when about four of her classmates had dragged her off and

[33]

hoisted her triumphantly into the air while the band burst into the school song for about the fiftieth time that day —

"The neurologist was pleased, huh?" Howard persisted.

J.P. considered him for a moment. "I'd like you to visit us often, Howard."

"Sure. Every day, if you want."

Howard had not really meant this, but Berenson nodded.

"Life must proceed normally. Every day would be fine. And I'll be grateful, as you'll discover."

He stroked Carol's hair again; he seemed relieved that she permitted him to do this.

"She does seem calmer," he said.

The convoy, with its motorcycle escort, had almost reached the high point of the canyon when a truck appeared — coasting downhill towards Sunset.

Carol saw it as it drew level with the Rolls. Her head turned from the window; her hands flew to her face. Berenson reached out for her as she gasped, choked, whimpered and twisted violently from side to side. He held her against him, tried to soothe her, while looking desperately around for some possible cause —

Howard kept repeating, "What is it? What is it?" and neither of them thought of the truck which (driven by an elderly Mexican and containing one hundred cases of California Chablis) trundled on by.

The chauffeur had pulled to the side; the nurse had braked, jumped out of the Pacer and joined them; the highway patrolmen had stopped traffic in both directions. Howard and the nurse watched as Berenson cradled his daughter, calming her, and telling her that there was nothing, nothing in this whole world that she needed to fear.

Eventually she calmed down. J.P. picked up the dark glasses, which had fallen onto the floor, and put them into his pocket. He nodded to the chauffeur, who waved to the highway patrolmen. The nurse — somewhat awed — returned to her car and the journey resumed.

J.P. took out his handkerchief and wiped Carol's face as she lay, ashen-white and sweating, against his shoulder.

"I'll make you well again," he told her — and the way he spoke carried the weight of a sacred pledge. "I'll make you well if it takes all my life and everything I own."

Howard turned away. He could not bear to look at J.P. at that moment.

Then the Rolls swung left off Benedict and disappeared through the towered gatehouse of Avonhurst.

BOOK
TWO

14

One year after these events (I have reconstructed them at last — from tapes, confidences, confessions)
the music of Steve Rice ushered me into Los Angeles.

It seemed to be playing everywhere: on radios, records and
tape decks, in cars, shops and hotels — the latest album (*Self-
Made Man*), which had already climbed to third place in the
all-time world charts.

We had been touring for six weeks, but even so, nothing
had prepared me for this; to be projected from London to
California at all was startling enough, but to arrive with Steve,
a part (however ill-defined) of his entourage was rather like
entering Rome with Caesar: for L.A. really had become the
rock capital. More records were cut here than anywhere, and
the true superstars were no longer film actors, but musicians.
The ailing movie industry with its vicissitudes and crises, its
vulnerability to television, its occasional hits subsidizing its
inevitable disasters, was being elbowed aside by a multi-
million-dollar business which simply grew and grew.

Rock music had achieved the dubious status of number one
world sales medium. The true roots of jazz, the blues, country
and folk had bled away and coagulated into a gross enterprise
whose influence upon vast crowds of people was approached
only by soccer. At the peak of this monolith sat the Disneyland
of the stars themselves — a capricious, druggy world in which
one four-minute song could make you rich for life; an in-
cestuous world with its own newspapers, its own vocabulary

(of about fifty words) and its own power structure revolving around the magic few, the rock elite — millionaire gods of the numerically largest generation in history.

From the start Steve had held himself aloof — an envied enigma within his own profession; too much the genuine loner to mingle on any more than a studio level, and too much of a cockney realist to share their Olympian dreams. Yet another refugee from that unlikely breeding ground of rock luminaries, the British working class, he had seen music from the start as a means of escape; a way out from under. Born (the year of "Heartbreak Hotel") into an impenetrably gloomy immigrant area of Brixton, in South London, his first guitar (acquired the year of *Sgt. Pepper's Lonely Hearts Club Band*) carried all the symbolic punch of Ali's first gloves.

He began to write songs, lilting and romantic at first, but unsentimental even then: there had always been a touch of Brixton anarchy. At sixteen he was playing the clubs, at eighteen he signed his first recording contract, and at twenty he was the second-highest-paid performer in the world. There were several reasons for this. The compositions themselves had become more persuasive with the years, the lyrics reflecting his own far-from-profound but deeply felt views on politics, racialism, religion and love. His voice, rough and fragile at the same time, was weirdly addictive — as were his stage performances. Steve was even better live than on records, and no one could deny his power to mesmerize audiences — the multitudes who sat before him silent and reverent and apparently oblivious of the fact that he hardly knew they were there. For one fact was unarguable — Steve played for himself alone. The fans mirrored him, nothing more, and they knew it and they did not care. They asked and expected nothing beyond the privilege of listening and staring —

Because finally Steve's looks were the most potent factor of all: slender, pale yet vividly alive, the mane of golden hair tossed in the halo of light, the microphone cord entwined in long fingers while he poured forth his songs of love and death . . . Steve truly reaped everyone, male and female. The gods had given him too much, and I have yet to meet an individual who remained indifferent.

Certainly no one in the Hollywood screening room where we had all assembled just two hours after landing by Lear jet from Denver.

15

After six weeks of live performances it felt odd to be watching Steve on film — especially as he sat next to me, totally absorbed while the camera craned from long to high shot, panned briefly to include the four-man backup group, then zoomed in to its loving close shot of his own fragile, aesthetic face.

The opening number ended to tumultuous on-screen applause; a caption appeared (STEVE RICE IN L.A.) then faded, to be replaced by a closeup of Howard Vance speaking straight into the camera:

"My name is Howard Vance and that was the start of a film I made of last year's Steve Rice concert at the Amphitheater — our most successful musical event since the Beatles first played the Hollywood Bowl. Today, one year later, the British star is back in town for the release of his new album *Reflections* — and to conclude his American tour with a free concert at the Forum. The film you are about to see is a chronicle of this visit to our city, by one of the foremost musical figures of our time."

The screen went blank, and a voice called "Cut!" I looked off to the left, to where Howard had been directing Joey, his cameraman, to film us watching his movie. The houselights came on, and there was a burst of applause from the invited audience of music-trade writers, reviewers, fan magazine editors, disc jockeys and publicists. Howard stepped in front of the screen.

"Well, that's how it starts."

Flashbulbs were popping now, and the notebooks were out.

"And we'll end with film of next month's concert, thereby forming a pleasing circular shape." Howard smiled around. "In between, there's footage of the tour, which I don't need to tell you has broken records clear across the country."

More applause — and I could understand their euphoria. Everyone involved with Steve was making so much money. (Even me, and all I had to do was jot things down.) For my own enlightenment, I had spent weeks pondering the economics of touring: how this one-man band could go on the road with seventy-five tons of equipment, a tour bill of two million dollars, a crew of sixty and still make fortunes bewildered me. I added up the pyramids of lights, the four hundred thousand watts of power needed to light the show, the thirty-five men who worked full time transporting seventy thousand pounds weight of electrical equipment across America in six forty-four-foot articulated trucks; the stage itself, sixty feet high, wide and deep, and so complex that it had taken twelve riggers three weeks to prepare one night for us in Chicago; the million dollars' worth of public-address system, weighing ten tons, plus two rows of Boeing-747 aircraft landing lights, which provided a blinding curtain of white heat, enough to burn the clothes off your back; then there was the promoting, the marketing, the jet planes, the film gear — the list was endless. And all for the presentation of a lone, plaintive singer from Brixton whose only true nostalgia was for the days when his singing dates involved packing a guitar and catching a train from Waterloo.

"Plus the L.A. footage," Howard was saying, "which I'll shoot in the studios, in the streets, wherever we happen to be. Steve finally said yes, and boy is Milton Rubin mad!"

Everyone laughed. I glanced at Steve, who smiled vaguely from the depths of his seat.

Howard continued: "You all know I was kind of dependent on Milton last year, but that's changed. This year I'll produce the film and the album myself."

They all clapped. Whatever the roots of Howard's new-found independence, there was no doubt that he was on his way up in a town where success (like failure) was seen as contagious: everyone wanted to know him.

"Now I'd like you to meet two newcomers to L.A. — Dave and Kathy Fryer. Dave's our resident playwright, and he's sitting there beside Steve. He's left the BBC in London to help us with some instant dialogue — in case our spontaneity dries up! He's also made a logbook of the tour, so please check Dave for background rather than the local press — that way the stories won't get too wild."

Howard smiled at me, and I smiled back. Where does your confidence come from? I wondered. Standing there in your custom-made Levi's, calling all the shots?

"And there's his wife Kathy —"

Kathy was on the other side of Steve. She stood up, turned, waved and sat down again. Her hair was auburn and she wore jeans tucked into high-heeled boots, and a suede blazer. She leaned forwards and smiled at me. I smiled back. I do not think she had any idea of how much I loved her.

"Kathy's working for us too, and single-handedly saved Vance Enterprises from chaos in London last summer. She's here to answer questions, specifically about the *Reflections* album, which she's been on from the start. So, that's it. Queries on the album to Kathy, queries on the tour to Dave."

And queries on life? On our future? To whom should they be addressed? To Howard, I supposed. He was certainly in the best position to answer them now: now that he was sleeping with Kathy again.

16

An enormous pink Cadillac, custom-built in
the late thirties, cruised past the Formosa restaurant on Santa
Monica and stopped outside the studio. It was followed by
three Mercedeses and an LASO squad car.

By the time Kathy and I reached the blinding heat of the
sidewalk there was a crowd of T-shirted fans around Steve,
and he had only made it halfway to the car. We stood with
Joey, the cameraman, on the studio steps for a moment while
Steve signed autographs. There was a lot of noise and jokes
and pushing and shoving but the security men had it all in
hand. Howard was sitting in the Cadillac, behind J.P. Berenson's chauffeur. He kept glancing at his watch.

"Great car," I remarked.

"Howard says it's bulletproof," said Kathy, blinking in the
light. "And it was built for John D. Rockefeller. But you know
Howard."

"Yes, I do."

I pulled a battered Robt. Burns cigar from my shirt pocket.
I had resisted smoking in the screening room — people always
complained.

"What does that mean?"

I lit the cigar rather shakily, from a book of matches entitled
"Ma Maison."

"It means if you're screwing Howard again, I'll go."

"Oh, don't be so ridiculous!"

She took out a pair of dark glasses and put them on. Joey
edged her sideways, trying for a better shot.

"Don't be such a bloody fool."

But she did not look at me, and I did not expect her to. Kathy could never look at you and lie at the same time. Some girls can, and some cannot. We used to grade them that way in the days before it mattered. But still I felt relieved and even grateful that she had bothered to lie at all. Something must be left.

She moved away, and down a couple of steps — past Joey. I joined her, speaking gently now.

"You got involved in London, I know —"

"We'd still be there without him, wouldn't we? In Fulham, watching the rain come down, with you carrying on about how everything happens in L.A. Of course I got involved, I work for him! I don't have to screw everyone I'm involved with."

Joey called suddenly: "Is that girl going to rape Steve?"

As I turned, a very pretty blonde in new, forty-five-dollar French jeans and a modified halter top with an inch of tummy showing had hurled both arms around Steve's neck and was kissing him passionately on the mouth, tongue and all.

"Son of a bitch!" Joey was filming furiously.

Steve disentangled himself and a security man in tennis clothes hauled the girl off. Both of her breasts soared clear of the halter top in the process, and a bearded man in a "Save the Whales" T-shirt fondled them while the girl was being set down.

Everyone laughed except Steve, who shook his golden hair angrily, said something to the bodyguards and turned towards the Cadillac.

"Hard to please, isn't he?" said the cameraman.

"Nobody likes being grabbed, Joey," said Kathy.

"Are you kidding? By a girl like that?" Joey was still filming the topless teenager. "He didn't even get her number. Hey, Mike?" he yelled to his assistant.

As Steve pushed his way towards the Cadillac, the crowd

regrouped, blocking him again. Kathy and I walked down the steps.

"I'm involved with Steve too, you know?"

"Yes."

"D'you think I'm screwing him?"

"Oh, Kathy —"

"Well, why not? Don't you think I fancy him?"

"I'm sure you do," I said tiredly. "The whole world fancies Steve."

Kathy looked at me in silence for a moment, her eyes impenetrable behind the dark glasses. Then suddenly she smiled. "Oh come on, let's have a drink!"

She called to Joey and pointed to a bar next to the screening room. He nodded, and went on filming.

17

The room was cool, dark, mahogany brown and lined with signed photographs of 1930s film stars. It was also empty: a leftover from the great days of Hollywood. A wave of cold air hit us as we walked in, and we sank into leather chairs by a window overlooking the sunbaked hubbub of the street.

Kathy picked up a monogrammed ashtray, considered it, set it down again. "I don't understand you. After eight years —"

"Nine."

"What?"

"Nine years."

"After nine years, why are you suddenly like this?"

"I don't know."

"And I was always the jealous one." Kathy shook her head. "When you were laying everything at the BBC —"

"Oh, come on —"

"Oh yes, all those horizontally minded secretaries. Did I ever threaten to leave?"

"No." I paused. "Perhaps you should've done."

"I'd never threaten, anyway." She shrugged.

"I know. You'd just go. And not from jealousy either. I worry now that you're not jealous."

Kathy considered the ashtray again.

"You've changed so much," I said.

She sighed. "Dave, we are both thirty-five years old."

"You're thirty-four."

"If we don't change now, we never will. Nothing happens,

does it? Our lives just — pass! In between the telly and the kitchen sink and your mother on Tuesdays and mine on Sundays and England's dead and London's had it and if only we could get to California, right? And now this! Our chance — to come to L.A., not like two bums who've saved up, but really come in style. By Lear jet. With our own personal superstar."

"Let's hope we survive it," I said.

An elderly waitress appeared. She wore a Marie Antoinette milkmaid's outfit which buttoned down the front.

"What can I get you folks?"

I looked at Kathy. "Wine?"

She nodded.

"Do you have any cold white wine?" I asked.

"Why sure, honey," replied the waitress, deadpan. "Hot white wine's just awful, isn't it? I have a friend who gave a hot white wine party last week and nobody came at all."

She chuckled; it was probably her favorite joke. Then she peered past us, out of the window.

"What's the attraction?"

"Steve Rice," I replied.

"Oh, him," she shrugged. "You know, I once saw Clark Gable mobbed on that very spot? Now he was an attraction."

"I agree," said Kathy.

"But Steve Rice?" The waitress gave a snort. "D'you know I read somewhere that jerk earns more in an hour than I do in a year?"

A teenaged colleague joined her at the window.

"Who is it?"

"Some kind of faggoty British singer."

The girl, who was on tiptoe for a better view, suddenly saw Steve. Her eyes widened, her mouth fell open.

"Jesus Christ!"

"Whatever you say, dear."

The girl dashed to the door, flung it open and hurled herself bodily into the crowd.

[49]

"What do they see in the spindly creep?" inquired the waitress.

"Don't you think he's pretty?" asked Kathy.

"Oh sure, so was Hedy Lamarr." She waved at the wall of photographs. "But take a look at those guys — are they pretty?"

Kathy considered a line of thirties idols.

"I think Gary Cooper's beautiful," she said.

"But he was a man, dear. A great big man. They don't want that now. They want boys. Boys who look like girls." She glanced around and lowered her voice confidentially. "I don't know why they don't just stay home and play with themselves!"

She paused, nodded significantly, and turned on her heel.

"Two cold Chablis coming up."

She marched off to the kitchen. I looked at Kathy. "So, the whole world doesn't fancy him."

"Faggoty British singer?"

"Our own personal superstar — a spindly creep."

"You're delighted, of course."

"Why should I be?"

"Pure envy."

"Not at all," I said.

"Really? You wouldn't like to be mobbed on that particular spot?"

"I'd hate it. On any spot."

"I'd love every moment of it. Fending off the fans." She looked at me and smiled. "You're going to tell me how I've changed again."

I shook my head. "I was thinking of Steve — maybe he shouldn't fend them all off. I mean, this faggoty image —?"

"He doesn't."

"What?"

"He doesn't fend them all off."

[50]

I paused. "Are you telling me that Steve's made it with a groupie?"

"In New York."

"How, I mean — did you watch?"

"No darling. But I saw him go off with her. A skinny little thing, who could hardly speak she was so impressed —"

"Oh yes," I interrupted. "Mousy hair and a sort of violet dress?"

Kathy looked at me.

"Do you know who that was? The television MC's daughter. And do you know where he took her? Onto the roof of the hotel where he read poetry in the moonlight — *The Waste Land*, by T.S. Eliot, of which she understood not one word. Then straight home to Dad. I heard it all next day. It's in my log of the tour."

Kathy paused:

"What's wrong with that?"

"Nothing. But it doesn't exactly help the faggoty image."

"Well, Steve's not gay."

"Are you sure?"

"Quite sure."

"How can you be?"

"Oh, all right," she sighed. "I'm not sure. But I have an instinct — like those girls out there."

"Don't get angry."

"I'm not angry. Anyhow, when you've sold a hundred million records, who cares about the image?"

"Maybe he does."

"Since when have you worried about Steve?"

"I like him, you'll be amazed to hear. I wouldn't have joined this circus otherwise."

Kathy found this hard to believe:

"You wouldn't?"

"No."

"You'd've let me come alone?"

"If you wanted."

"And missed it all? Yes, I think you would! You don't see the chances. You don't see anything! Or else you see everything except what matters."

I was not sure whether to welcome this outburst or not. I knew that we were so near to the end, and this was the first time we had talked in weeks, since New York really, and I did not want to stop. There is always hope, I told myself, while the dialogue lasts. Something miraculous might emerge, some forever unspoken thought that would point me the way back; or I might even stumble upon something myself, some magic combination of words to surprise the feelings back into that beautiful face. I regarded her now, with the same joy as always: she had not aged one bit, and when she returned my gaze it was all the same, the mouth, the eyes, only the love had gone. A ghost-girl. A total stranger, of whom everything was known. I had to look away.

"What does matter, Kathy?"

"You do."

"Just me?"

"Your career. You're a marvellous writer but nobody knows it."

"Some epitaph."

"What?"

" 'He was a marvellous writer, but nobody knew it.' "

"Oh well, if we're into epitaphs —"

"I'm sorry."

"You're your own worst enemy, Dave. You don't have to write crap. It's not as if I don't work. You're too good to tart up other people's scripts. You've got to break out of it now, we both have. And L.A.'s the place."

I almost said, "Without you there is no place." I could have said that easily but it would have sounded trite and maudlin and she would have been embarrassed or forced to lie, or both. It never helps to say things like that, in my experience, even if you mean them. Especially if you mean them. The sad truth is that remarks like that only work, only dissolve the other person, precisely when you do not mean them. The more you care the better advised you are to shut up and hope for the best, I find.

"Why do you think all our friends are here?" she went on. "Everyone we knew? Half the people who came to our wedding are in L.A. It's like Sloane Square, 1968."

Would to God, I thought. The Golden Age: the one you never know you are living through. And that was the crux of it, of course — Kathy's urgent feeling for the passage of time. I rarely gave it a thought myself because — suffering as I do from a chronic sense of unreality, I always imagine everything will go on forever. (Intellectually of course I know it will not — but somehow I always imagine that it will, and so am permanently surprised by endings.)

"And I was always the ambitious one," I said. "I was ambitious, and you were jealous. We've switched roles, you and I — like in experimental drama."

"What's wrong with that?"

"Just that they always end so weirdly, those plays."

"You're obsessed with endings, aren't you? Try a few beginnings, for a change."

A rush of warm air from the street heralded the return of the teenaged waitress, clutching a crumpled piece of paper. She looked flushed and dishevelled, her milkmaid's top all askew.

"Did you get his autograph?" asked Kathy.

"Oh sure — I just hope I didn't get pregnant at the same time."

She pulled at the ripped threads of her missing buttons.

"To get anywhere near him you gotta be felt up by eight hairy freeloaders in sweatshirts!"

She hurried off to the kitchen. I glanced out at the street. The fans had multiplied, and the sexual parasites around

Steve were having a field day. I remembered one time in Chicago when there had been so many girls jamming the foyer of his hotel that a quite famous rock group had driven over especially to siphon them off.

"Well, at least she got his autograph," I remarked.

We watched the crowd for a moment longer, then saw Joey waving to us and pointing to the Cadillac. We rose immediately. I opened the large wallet I had taken to carrying, dropped a note onto the table, and followed Kathy out of the bar.

Outside, I looked back and saw our waitress through the window. She set the Chablis at our table, pocketed the five dollars, then stared out at the street. She saw me, and waved suddenly. Then she picked up a glass, turned, raised it — I imagine to Gary Cooper — and drank.

18

"Fucking 'ell, you might've warned me!" said Steve from the back seat of the Cadillac.

J.P. Berenson's chauffeur turned, startled as people always were by a speaking voice so at odds with appearance: somehow no one expected those flat cockney vowels to emerge from the face of an angel.

"I told you yesterday, and again today." Howard sounded harassed. He was sitting beside Steve. Kathy and I had climbed in front with the chauffeur. Joey and the security men were a couple of Mercedeses behind.

"I'd've put on dungarees and a crash 'elmet." Steve was examining a deep tear in his hand-embroidered voile shirt.

"We need a mob scene, and that was it. Let's go, Ace." This last was to the chauffeur, who was still staring at Steve.

Ace turned, engaged gear, and hooted the horn. The patrolmen had managed to clear the road ahead, but there were still faces pressed against the back and side windows as we moved off, leading the convoy west along Santa Monica.

Howard switched on the stereo (another track from the *Self-Made Man* LP) and gave the air conditioning a boost. We gathered speed, and the last bobbing head moved off and away. I looked back at the running, waving crowd. There was something about them, their gleaming eyes, their worshipful air, that always moved me. I find mankind's urge for Christ substitutes second only to its need for child substitutes in pathos.

"Those heavies are useless too," said Steve. "All they did was grab asses out there."

"They're human, Steve," replied Howard, making light of it. He pulled open the chrome drinks-cabinet, and selected two cut-glass tumblers.

"They're sub 'uman. Get rid of them."

Howard paused. "But I've only just hired them —"

"Then unhire them. I don't want them around."

Howard looked at him. It was rare for Steve to speak at all, let alone assert himself. Mostly he just swallowed pills, read T.S. Eliot, and daydreamed. We had grown accustomed to this pale, withdrawn creature coming alive only on stage — if then. It was an event to see him angry. Howard sighed, and dropped ice into the glasses.

"The honest truth is, I'm to blame. I asked them to let a couple of girls through — for Joey, you know? For the movie —"

"Did you also ask them to feel up all those kids out there?"

"Well no, of course not —"

"Why should they 'ave to be assaulted to get near me?"

"Look, Steve, you need security —"

"If I ever see those randy apes again you can forget the L.A. footage, all right?"

"All right, " said Howard quickly. "Calm down. You won't see them again."

There was a cracking of ice as Howard poured on the scotch.

I glanced at Kathy, who gave a little facial shrug which said stay out of it. But it is true, I thought, I really did like Steve. He always surprised me; whenever I dismissed him as the egomaniac of all time, he would come up with the unexpected — in this case a completely dispassionate concern for his fans, mixed with a paranoid loathing of bully-boys, dating back to God knows what childhood traumas on the playground of Brixton Grammar School.

Also, in spite of all the pressures and the touring and the hero worship, he had never changed (though why I should place such value on continuity, I do not know). Christ substitute or not, Steve was truly indifferent to his fame. He had never sought it. Deification had been thrust upon him, and had given him nothing in return that he valued. I would say that he had contempt for fame, but that is too strong a word. He cared as little for it as he did for security, money, or sex. Or for anything at all, in fact, which existed outside that classical brow. He was linked to the world through music alone, and I suppose that at this point he had travelled about as far from what is currently defined as reality as it was possible (short of being actually certifiable) for a man to do.

Howard passed him a drink, and I reflected that of course these qualities did not make a producer's job any easier. For example, I knew that Steve's refusal to talk to the press had driven Howard practically insane in London. (Steve had given one interview at the age of seventeen, when a misquote of his views on Bob Dylan had so enraged him that he had vowed never to address a journalist again.)

He was equally dismissive of television, and although the media had managed to trap him at Kennedy on our arrival in New York six weeks before, they had drawn very little out of him beyond a few smiles and the occasional ambiguous quip. He had managed to make himself more mysterious than ever, and although snide articles dubbing him "The Garbo of Rock" had annoyed the New York promoter, they had no apparent effect on Steve — assuming he even read them, which I doubt.

"You've got security at Avonhurst, anyhow," Ace was saying.

"Did Kellerman come through?" asked Howard.

"Four cops on the gate, plus the Bel Air patrol. Also, no one gets in without personalized invitations and IDs."

Howard nodded, yawned, drank and stared out of the window.

We were on Sunset now, heading for Benedict Canyon. We

had passed through the bright, bold poster colors of the Strip — dotted with billboards showing Steve's face sixteen feet high — and were now crossing the manicured drives of Beverly Hills, where no one walked. Water sprinklers sprayed on all sides, and I remembered the talk of fires in the canyons, of mutilated trees and vegetation. The street temperature was ninety-two and rising.

We stopped at some lights just before Benedict, and then pulled away past a graceful pink-and-white building, fringed by palms.

"What's that place?" Steve inquired.

"The Beverly Hills Hotel," replied Howard, patiently. Then, unable to resist it: "You stayed there for a month last year."

Steve turned and contemplated the hotel. Then he shrugged, took a flat enamel box from his shirt pocket, opened it, flipped a blue tablet into his mouth and downed it with the scotch.

"I hear they're bringing out a pill for the memory soon," Howard said.

19

Ace spun the wheel and we turned right, onto Benedict Canyon. He revved as the gradient rose, and gently shifted gears.

"A great car," I remarked.

"They don't make them like this," said Ace.

"Is it really bulletproof?"

"Built for Guggenheim in 1938. George Guggenheim, the one who shot himself. It's Mr. Berenson's favorite."

As the pink Cadillac led our cavalcade along the canyon, a big traffic jam was building up by the entrance to Hillcrest Drive. We joined the end of the line, behind a battered Thunderbird driven by a dazzling blonde. The bumper sticker read AMERICA — LOVE IT OR LEAVE IT.

"What's the holdup, Ace?" called Howard.

"Could be another fire."

This observation was followed by the deafening shriek of sirens — the paranoiac American-police-car clamor — and Ace edged us farther over to the right as three LAPD squad cars and an ambulance unit roared past on the wrong side of the road.

Howard got out of the car and stared after them, but there was nothing to see except other motorists doing the same. He called to Steve, pointedly:

"I'm going back to talk to the randy apes."

Steve pulled out his battered paperback of *Collected Poems* by T.S. Eliot and settled back to read.

I turned to watch as Howard walked along our convoy of

cars, and saw that Joey — never one to miss a spontaneous event — was already out with his camera. He ran past us and on among the jostling crowd at the sealed-off entrance to the drive; he questioned a few people, and then shot some more feet of California crowd behavior.

Kathy opened the door and called, "What is it, Joey?"

"No one knows. Some kind of accident maybe."

At that point two more squad cars appeared over the hill from the direction of Mulholland and swung right through the police cordon and onto Hillcrest Drive.

"Too much brass around for an accident," said Ace.

Then we all fell silent and sat contemplating the scene ahead; the controlled confusion, the unexplained chaos and suddenly, I do not know why, I felt my first shiver of fear.

Since the moment of our arrival in California it had been there — behind the apparent serenity — this almost tangible sense of violence. Initially, I had put it down to the lines of energy, the sheer, total thrust of the place; but not anymore. That surface was too bland to be true; it was a contrived, tranquillized calm, masking God knew what. These Angelenos were somehow too relaxed, with their sunshine and their music. I had the feeling that the most monstrous things in the world could happen in this state, with no warning at all, out of that perfect sky — and without even interrupting that great California beat for more than a moment.

So far the omens had been slight. Earlier that day I stood in the window of room 44 at the Chateau Marmont Hotel, waiting for Kathy to finish in the bathroom. I was looking down onto the sunlit Strip, where the traffic moved in gentle, ordered lines beneath the hand-painted billboards (L.A. drivers are rated second only to West Germans in obedience — a tribute to the zeal of the LAPD). Suddenly, with no warning, a black Chevrolet went berserk: lurched from its lane, bumped across the empty sidewalk and crashed sickeningly into a brick wall. It then reversed savagely across the four-lane street, narrowly missing an oncoming bus, hit the opposite curb, then roared forwards again, completing its suicidal three-point turn by demolishing a streetlamp. At last it stopped. Nobody got out. The traffic maneuvered around it with great circumspection. As I watched, people emerged from bars and shops and strolled towards the car. When Kathy came out of the bathroom I pointed down, but there was not much to see, just a black car out of alignment with the others; and, as we were late for Howard's screening, I never found out what happened. Had the driver simply gone mad? Was it the heat, or drugs? More than anything, why had the incident affected me so? Something to do with the suddenness, I supposed. The brief, sudden outrage of it —

Ten minutes later Kathy and I stood in a glass-walled Hertz office on La Cienega, while a clerk completed the documentation on the Volkswagen we were to use during our visit. This time it was Kathy who noticed a blazing Corvette in the street. You had to look quite closely to make out the flames at all, because the surrounding sunlight burned almost as brightly as the car. I presumed there was no one inside, but in any case no one was doing anything. Occasionally, a passerby would stare — as if this disintegrating machine was some form of local artwork. I asked if anyone had called the fire department. The Hertz clerk said oh sure, and went on completing our documents. Finally there was a wailing siren, and a fire engine raced past the office without a pause. Oh look, remarked the clerk, he's gone right on past. Then he checked through the forms again. When we left, the Corvette still burned as fiercely as ever.

I sat in the pink Cadillac, thinking of what a friend had told me about L.A. It has no history, he said, no roots. It was simply dumped there, in the desert. And it is the most profoundly foreign place you will ever visit. You would feel more at home in Senegal or Beirut than you will in Los Angeles. It is a town in which everything you ever wanted will seem to be just around the corner, just out of sight — fame, money, love — but when you turn that corner what you will see will be something else again. But you will never forget L.A., and you may never recover from your visit. (City of the Fallen Angels! Thank God I did not know then how right he was.)

On Benedict Canyon Drive there was some movement at last. The two snakelike, multicolored streams of Saturday traffic inched towards each other, skirting the police roadblock with its flashing lights at the entrance to Hillcrest Drive, and resumed their winding parallel courses up and down the canyon.

Howard climbed back in, slamming the door.

"I've fired the gorillas. We'll have to pay them anyhow." He undid several buttons on his shirt. He was sweating. "Also, there's been a landslide in the Valley."

"This sure is one hell of a summer," said Ace.

20

The towered gatehouse of Avonhurst is a
two-storied affair, punctured by a single archway, set back a
hundred yards from Benedict Canyon Drive. Our convoy
(now minus the security-men's Mercedeses) was expected, and
we passed through what I guessed to be a complex electronic
surveillance system without delay. Armed men waved from
a window, then vanished.

The journey across the estate, from the gatehouse to the
castle itself, took over ten minutes, and by the end of it even
Steve had laid down his book and was paying attention, for
we had entered a domain: a unique, totally private world, an
eighteenth-century Claude landscape set high in the hills
overlooking Bel Air, which overlooked Beverly Hills, which
looked down upon L.A.

As we travelled up the winding, statue-punctuated central
drive, I stared out at broad paths leading to avenues which
stretched clear away to the skyline. There were formal plan-
tations juxtaposed with paths through deep groves and wil-
dernesses; as the Cadillac dipped and rose we crossed a
Palladian bridge, glimpsed a crumbling mock-ruin in the
shape of a tower, looked down at brooks, wooded glades,
pools, canals, cascades — and groups of dark-eyed gardeners
who stared silently back at us. These were descendents of the
armies of long-dead Mexicans who had labored for years
upon this land, levelling it and transplanting vast acres of

pine forest — Mediterranean pines, light as a bird's feather — the silvery olive orchards, the mimosas, the cypresses, the majestic cedars and oaks. Offending houses on surrounding land had been bought up and demolished in the twenties. Valleys had been cut through intervening slopes, permitting the eye to roam uninterrupted over wide stretches of green. At every turn was some new surprise — an obelisk or an archway or some strange, heraldic statue; and each discovery led to some further view, to some yet further dimension of the estate.

"The statues all came from Greece," volunteered Ace, as we came to a fork in the central drive. He veered right, and continued:

"There's a Spanish chapel down there, and a Holy Well and a monk's garden, and everything. This way there's a Japanese pavilion. Mr. Berenson used to travel a lot."

The drive wound through a pine forest, dipped a little, then emerged from the trees. I stared at the far hills: they were gray-blue, above the green crown of pines. We came to a lake, as smooth as glass, fed by a stream which wound gently beneath drooping willows.

"It was all scrubland before," Ace told us. "Just to irrigate it costs more than we'll ever see."

I shook my head. To me there was something disturbing, even manic about this converted wasteland. The lyricism of a pastoral European landscape transposed to the desert — for what? What monumental ego was thereby satisfied? (God said Let there be flowers, and there were flowers.)

Beyond the lake, the drive curled sharply away to the left and there suddenly, set amid palm trees and formal Italian gardens, stood the castle — its pointed arches gleaming in the sun. Nothing had prepared me for the overpowering presence of the place. I had expected Hollywood Romantic, or Marzipan Gothic, but this was neither: those casements and battlements were built of worn, glowing stones, older than the Republic itself. The chauffeur slowed down.

In the back of the car, Howard turned to Steve. "So, that's it. Maybe even you'll remember."

"All it needs is a Yellow Brick Road." But Steve's eyes were fully open for the first time that day.

I smiled, but did not agree. This was no castle of Oz, but a real house in which generations of real people had lived and died: the only mystery was how it came to be in California. Kathy turned, delighted as a child — half laughing, half marvelling.

"It was all shipped over stone by stone in the thirties," said Howard. "By J.P.'s father — Berenson senior."

That rang a bell. But really, so little has been written about Avonhurst compared with, say, San Simeon: because whereas Hearst had been a publicist, the Berensons were always reclusive, spending vast amounts on nonpublicity — on simply staying out of the newspapers. The drive made a double twist, then spiralled down into a gravel courtyard beside the castle. Several cars were already parked: a powder blue Rolls-Royce Corniche with strange license plates, a silver Jaguar, a VW bus and, somewhat surprisingly, a black-and-white LAPD squad car.

"Kellerman," muttered Ace.

We stopped beside the VW, and all got out. Ace began to unload our suitcases.

"They're probably all in the back," said Howard, and he hurried off towards a flamboyant archway covered with red bougainvillea.

We delayed for a moment, looking up at the soaring towers. The air was heavy with the scent of jasmine. Kellerman's driver glanced across, recognized Steve, and lowered his copy of *New West.* Joey's Mercedes arrived, and was backing in beside the Cadillac as we followed Howard through the archway. Our L.A. Sheriff's Office escort braked to a halt in the middle of the courtyard, and various detectives descended. They stood around talking. Kellerman's driver joined them.

There was an air of tension about these policemen — as if they knew something that we did not.

21

"It's happened again, Howard." Berenson's tone was neutral. "In Bel Air. This time it was a man, and they've killed him."

Howard stared at J.P., then around at us, unbelieving. We were hovering a few feet behind on a path leading from the courtyard; we were waiting to be introduced, but Howard was understandably sidetracked by the news.

"So that was the holdup —?"

"They found the body an hour ago. Kellerman's just told me."

I was looking at Berenson for the first time — the long gray hair, the dark impassive face. He stood barefoot beside a scarlet geranium bush — hands deep in the pockets of baggy cotton trousers.

Kellerman emerged from the castle and joined us. He carried a large manila envelope. Howard turned to him. "And you're really sure it's the same —?"

"The same type of duffel bag, with a note attached. Plus the *L.A. Times* delivery boy saw a truck pull out of Hillcrest at six this morning."

"A truck? Jesus, I thought you'd checked out every single — !"

"There are several million trucks in California." Kellerman sounded weary. "And who knows? They could've been in Mexico all this time."

"Jesus," repeated Howard.

"So now it's a homicide, and we have a witness. The boy will ID them. Plus we have more sketches —"

Kellerman withdrew three pencilled artist's impressions from the manila envelope and held them up. I saw them clearly: the first showed a thin-faced man, wearing a peaked cap; the second was round-faced, cherubic, in steel-framed spectacles; the third was hook-nosed, foreign-looking.

"These match exactly with the Salinas girl's description," said Kellerman.

"And who did they attack this time?" asked Howard.

"A homosexual. A hustler they could've picked up anywhere. The note said 'Lead us not into temptation.'" Kellerman shrugged, then turned to J.P. "So, I'll be in my office, and I'll send the girls down later. Thank you, sir."

He walked away through the archway. We all stood silently for a moment, then Howard spoke. "John, this is Steve Rice."

J.P. extended his hand. "Welcome to this violent place."

Steve shook the hand. J.P. considered him closely. "The superintendent has two daughters who are desperate to meet you. As a favor to him, I've invited them."

"Of course." Steve was on his best behavior.

"I don't think they'll ask for much. Just your autograph should suffice."

Howard turned to us. "And this is Dave and Kathy Fryer."

Confronting Berenson fully for the first time, I was immediately struck by his eyes: hooded, introspective, deep-set in the formal mask of his face.

"Thank you for coming."

He shook hands warmly enough — but I found his manner inscrutable even then. Relaxed yet distant: and how could I have guessed at the pressures at work upon him? (I must admit that even now, after everything has happened — things I never thought I would find the courage to write about — I understand J.P. no better than at the beginning: human nature baffles me more and more as I grow older. The simple

[68]

certainties are deserting me daily; the illusions are on the march, and perhaps it is just as well — I have enough emotional hand-baggage to carry through life without them.)

"This new assault is a shock for us all," he was saying. "It's the third inside a year. The second was on my daughter Carol, as you may know."

It was about all I did know. J.P. was immensely rich and had a crazy daughter who had once been engaged to Howard. She had been raped and beaten up the year before, and had not spoken since. She was still under psychiatric care, and no one knew her exact condition except Howard — who always refused to talk about it.

J.P. continued to regard us; neither Kathy nor I could think of much to say, but fortunately nothing seemed required, and Howard broke the pause —

"I need some shots of Steve in the courtyard, so we'll see you later." He turned towards the archway, where Joey was waiting.

"Lunch is at two, Howard," said J.P. "And maybe you'd show Mister Rice to his room?"

"Sure."

J.P. looked after Steve for a moment. "He seems a modest enough boy."

"To a fault," I said.

"That's Howard's biggest problem," Kathy added. "Getting him to perform offstage."

J.P. nodded, turned abruptly and led us towards the back of the castle.

22

If the approach to Avonhurst was eighteenth-century French the rear — with its Olympic-sized pool, floodlit tennis courts and Jaccuzis behind hedges — could not have been more California. We crossed a perfect lawn, interspersed with beach chairs, umbrellas, water sprinklers and deferential Mexican servants.

A white-jacketed majordomo emerged from the poolhouse, hurried over and spoke to Berenson, who shrugged and glanced at his watch. Kathy walked on ahead and paused — momentarily blinded by the pool. Shading her eyes, she gazed off into the distance, to where the rolling lawn pitched and twisted into a pine forest, enclosed by the electric fences of the estate. She turned and stared up at the soaring, fairy-tale grace of the castle itself, the Gothic windows glowing in the sun, then threw up her arms in a spontaneous gesture of delight.

I glanced at Berenson and saw that he was smiling. Kathy looked good enough at any time, but when she lit up like this, bursting with that marvellous enthusiasm which once I — and only I — could inspire, she was radiant.

J.P. sat opposite me on a chaise longue beside the pool. A striped umbrella cast a disc of shade across us. White-gloved servants converged. Drinks were poured. J.P. raised his glass.

"To your first visit to L.A."

I thanked him, surprised that he should know that — or anyway have remembered it. We drank. Kathy continued her tour of the pool.

"You have a charming wife," observed J.P. "I admire English women. Carol's mother came from Wiltshire."

"Kathy was born there too," I said.

"A beautiful county. It's also where my father found Avonhurst."

He sat regarding me, unsurprised by these coincidences.

"Are you divorced now?" I ventured.

"My wife died."

There was a little silence. I shifted in my chair and flicked some sweat from my forehead.

"This heat is unnatural," remarked J.P. "There will be an earthquake soon."

"Not this weekend, I hope?"

He smiled, but I could see that he was serious.

"Tremors have been recorded. Real estate is down."

Then I remembered that of course there had been earthquakes in California. I also had a sudden irrational notion that J.P. would be unconcerned — that a totally spontaneous natural disaster would not displease this man in any way.

"I want to thank you for inviting us —" I began.

"You are friends of Howard's," he interrupted. "And Howard has become like a son to me. Since Carol's illness he's visited whenever he was in town. That's a debt I never can repay."

I nodded. So that explained Howard's recent affluence, and the dumping of Milton Rubin.

Kathy joined us.

"And was it really all shipped over?" she asked.

"Stone by numbered stone," smiled J.P. "To impress a woman. She was also English." He nodded to me. "And said she would never live in California, she wanted a real country estate. So my father bought Avonhurst. But when she finally arrived she didn't like it. Oh no, she said, it's much too big. And she went away again. So he left the East Wing crated up in San Francisco, and gave up romantic gestures."

[71]

"And it all comes from Wiltshire," I told Kathy. "The whole place."

She turned to Berenson. "Perhaps that's why I feel so at home here."

"Do you?" he replied. "You don't find it too big?"

They both suddenly laughed, then fell silent. I watched a blue hummingbird hover above the pool, then drift away.

"And it will be good to see it full tonight!" added J.P. "Our last party was for Carol's eighth birthday, the year before her mother died. There were two hundred guests on this lawn and the kids wore fancy dress. We had fireworks, and a great barbecue." He smiled briefly at the memory. "But after that I rented places, hotels and restaurants, for Carol's celebrations."

"He's so grateful," said Kathy. "Howard I mean. To be able to bring everyone here —"

"He deserves it. Has he found his cover girl yet?"

"She's in Beverly Hills," replied Kathy. "Having her hair cut."

"And does she really look like Steve?"

"They could be twins. Or even 'Reflections' — like the album says. You'll see tonight."

"Is that when they meet?"

"Howard will introduce them in front of everyone. He wants a public response out of Steve — a meaningful human reaction, as he calls it!" Kathy turned to me. "Oh, and we've changed her name to Stephanie, don't you like that? Steve and Stephanie — his doppelgänger."

The majordomo appeared beside J.P. "Huey Stander is here, sir."

We all turned. Four men strolled across the lawn towards the poolhouse. One was tall, silver-haired, wearing a Pierre Cardin summer suit; the next two looked like brothers, in their early twenties, ash-blond bleached-haired surfers in Fred Segal jeans and Gucci loafers; the last was a wiry athlete with his hair tied back in a ponytail, bare chest gleaming above high-waisted bell-bottoms. They were all carrying tennis rackets and Adidas bags. The tall man waved.

J.P. stood up.

"That is my New York accountant. We'll meet at lunch. Please ask for anything you need."

He walked off to join the new arrivals. I looked at Kathy. "That's an accountant?"

Kathy shrugged, and stood up.

"I'm going to change," she said.

"I'll finish this drink."

She nodded, and crossed the lawn. At the south terrace she spoke to a servant, who smiled and led her through a carved doorway into the castle.

I leaned back in my chair and drew a couple of deep breaths. I was relieved to have a moment alone, if only to try to sort out my deepening sense of unreality and foreboding. What was it all about? Why was I getting these sudden sweats and cramps? Was I ill? Or allergic to heat? Of course I was in a state about Kathy, sick with fear at the thought of losing her: but why should that affect everything? After all, I was not going to lose her this weekend, so why not relax and enjoy this place, this host, and what was obviously going to be the party of the year? The thing to do, I told myself, was to climb into some shorts, smother myself with sun cream, and calm down.

I sat for a moment longer, watching a dark-skinned gardener prune some roses near the terrace. Beside him loomed a Giacometti statute: lean and solitary, image of isolation in the still heat.

I stared down at the burning stones beside the water; then across at the poolhouse itself, which was pure Los Angeles — Hockney Los Angeles — relating architecturally to the pool rather than to the castle; and there was J.P., standing in the shade, talking to his four guests. The tall man waved his arms expressively and laughed. He looked anything but an accountant; still, I had heard that in L.A. people rarely looked like what they were — dentists frequently resembling film stars and so forth. The ponytailed athlete was miming a tennis serve, his muscles rippling impressively. The bleached blonds stood with folded arms and pumped-up biceps, listening attentively to Berenson. It all seemed perfectly normal.

I finished my drink and stood up. I decided to walk once around the outside of the castle to get my bearings before going in to find Kathy. I set off in the opposite direction from the way we had come, towards the east side of the castle. Leaving the lawn, I followed a gravel path which zigzagged between tall trees like those of my childhood. A sudden snarling of dogs made me turn. Across a carved hedge I saw — pacing about behind a wrought-iron fence — two enormous German shepherds. I walked on, reflecting that anyway it would be odd to find a large estate without guard dogs.

The path curved between brilliantly flowering hedges, past trimmed shrubs and rustic seats decorated with twisted branches; finally it delivered me into a triangular clearing, where three paths met. In the center stood a green-and-white pole, topped by a unicorn in scarlet wood. I stopped, studying this heraldic object, remembering that I had seen one identical years before in England — in the King's garden at Hampton Court. (And considering this family's propensity for buying up whatever it fancied, this could well be the same one.)

At which point I felt someone watching me. I turned quickly, and there was a woman, standing beside a cypress tree.

She gazed back at me, her expression both remote and acutely sad. Her hair was gray, dank; her white face blotched and lined. Her pale dress hung loosely over her thin body; she looked middle-aged and sick. I paused, confused by this sudden apparition. Then, summoning a smile, I called —

"Hullo!"

"Hullo," she replied, with no emphasis whatsoever.

"My name's David."

"David."

"I was just admiring this statue. It's beautiful."

"Beautiful."

And, without another word, she walked on towards the castle.

I stood perplexed, watching her disappear along the gravel path, reflecting that there could be the cause of my unease. (The presence of nervous disorder has always affected me — our proximity to the local lunatic asylum even obliged my parents to move house once, reluctantly, in 1952.)

Not that the sad creature I had just seen was necessarily mad, but she was clearly disturbed —

As yet I did not realize she was Carol Berenson.

23

Inside the castle, Kathy was exploring.

A servant had escorted her to the head of a Palladian staircase, where he had politely indicated that her door was the
first to the left, and then gone about his duties. Seduced by
the several million dollars' worth of tapestries and paintings
hanging ahead however, Kathy had wandered down the corridor, turned right, then on up another deeply carpeted staircase (seventy-five wood-carvers had once labored for a year
on the balustrades alone). She entered a gilded library, lined
with rare books, and stared up at a magnificently painted
ceiling, imported from a Florentine palace.

It was as she passed through the library into a great hall
of statuary and marble that Kathy recalled (when we compared notes later) the first eerie sensation of being watched.
She glanced around, but failed to see Carol — who must have
crept in from the grounds and followed, gliding as wraithlike
among the statues as she had between the trees.

Kathy wandered through silk-walled rooms filled with
Chinese vases, Sèvres porcelain, antique silver. She paused,
savoring the booty of a lifetime — running her fingers along
Sheraton chairs, Dresden shepherdesses, lingering on a pale
jade leopard that had once enchanted the Emperor Ch'ien-
lung. Finally, turning from a painting by Breughel the Elder,
Kathy's attention was attracted by a dull pink glow emanating
from a door opposite. She pushed it open and paused, her
eyes wide.

Before her stretched the most extravagant fancy of Avon-hurst: an English version of the Hall of Mirrors at Versailles. On every wall hung eighteenth-century looking-glasses of the type designed by Adam and Chippendale — their carved and molded borders depicting birds, flowers and mythological subjects. An obelisk of glass pointed at the domed ceiling — which had itself been designed as half a dome, to be completed by its own reflection. Tiers of mirrors, decreasing in size, lined the ceiling, throwing out a wild mélange of shapes and colors — swirling pinks from the Persian carpet, brown and gold from the mouldings.

Multiple images of Kathy moved cautiously into the room, and a cockney voice spoke:

"What do you think of it so far?"

Kathy almost collapsed with fright, and then saw Steve. He was sitting on a couch at the far end of the room.

"Come over 'ere," he said.

Several hundred tall skinny girls crossed the mirrored hall and sat beside him. He pointed to a fluted, multiangled glass. "What do you see in there?"

Kathy gazed into the mirror for a moment, then replied, "I see myself."

"Just yourself?"

"Sitting beside myself on this couch."

"I'm not there at all?"

"No." She paused. "You're not a vampire, by any chance?"

"It's the same for me."

"It's a good trick."

"Or else the truest mirror on earth."

After a moment:

"What would happen if we touched each other?" asked Steve.

"I've often wondered," smiled Kathy, who was taking all this more lightly than he was.

"Maybe it would just look as if we were touching ourselves?"

He raised his right hand to Kathy's face. She looked directly at him.

In the mirror: images of Steve caressing himself — curving back to infinity.

Then, a sharp intake of breath. Steve turned.

A movement in the doorway, and Carol was gone.

"What the fuck was that?"

He lowered his hand, startled.

Carol ran as fast as she could, sobbing and gasping along galleries and passages until she reached a brighter, more modern wing of the castle. She flung herself into her own room, slamming the door behind her.

24

I had decided to ask J.P. about the vision by the cypress tree, and so I returned to the lawn.

There were towels and sandals scattered around the pool now, and the blond surfers were frolicking in the water, stark naked except for identical turquoise necklaces. The pony-tailed athlete was lying on a crimson towel, sunbathing — also nude except for white tennis socks. I wondered if we were in for a full-frontal afternoon, which I always find rather embarrassing, or if they would at least cover their cocks when Kathy appeared. I had to admit, in passing, that they all seemed in great physical shape.

Berenson was sitting on the verandah, still deep in conversation with Huey; the sun reflected dazzlingly from the sliding glass doors behind him. They both paused as I approached.

"I'm sorry to bother you —"

Berenson looked attentive.

"But I've just met a woman in your grounds who seemed, uh — troubled, and —"

"Whereabouts?"

"In the clearing with the scarlet unicorn —"

J.P. rose immediately.

"Was she alone?"

"Yes."

"Thank you. That was my daughter. It's a favorite spot of hers. Huey, this is Dave Fryer. I'll see you at lunch." He nodded to me, and walked away across the lawn.

[79]

"His daughter?"

"You didn't know?" asked Huey.

"Well, I knew he had a daughter, but —"

"Have a drink. There's scotch, tequila, California Chablis —"

"I mean, how old is she?"

"Nineteen. Looks fifty, doesn't she? It's a terrible thing. Try the tequila."

"Thanks." I was still absorbing this information. "I thought she couldn't speak?"

"She couldn't. But now she can. That is, she can speak but she can't say anything. All she can do is repeat what you tell her, like some poor demented parrot."

I sat down rather heavily on the canvas chair vacated by J.P.

"There's even a medical name for it — 'echolalia' it's called. Consequence of shock and possible lesions of the brain. Ice?"

"What?"

"Do you take ice?"

"Oh, yes —"

He dropped ice into the tequila.

"I think you'll enjoy this."

I thanked him, and drank. It was strong, but pleasant. I felt a little better. I looked across at the pool, to where a great deal of splashing and horseplay had begun. Huey smiled at me.

"What's a nice British boy like you doing in a place like this?"

"I wish I knew."

"We're screening some of Howard's film after lunch — I'm looking forward to that. Also to meeting Steve Rice. What do you think of him?"

"I never know how to answer that."

Huey raised his eyebrows.

"He's a very private man," I added.

"Is he as beautiful offstage as on?"

"So they say."

"And you have no personal view? I can't believe it!" he chuckled. "Look at those idiots —"

One of the surfers had just dived in off the side of the pool, caught hold of the other's air mattress, and tipped him over. The sunbathing athlete yelled complaints about the splashing, and hurled tennis balls at the spluttering brothers.

"How'd you like to be twenty again?"

I shrugged. "I had a rotten time at twenty."

"Well, maybe you chose the wrong year for it. I think now would be good." He stood up. "Listen, I have to get out of this suit. Come and talk to me. Bring your drink."

He waited for me.

"A private man, you say? That's interesting."

Huey dropped his Vuitton holdall on the floor of the poolhouse and removed his jacket. I looked around at the air-conditioned interior: telephones; TV sets; hand-painted tiles; Mexican rugs; cactus plants; rails of towels; racks of sun cream and tennis balls; yellow shower curtains; low beds covered with the tangled jeans, T-shirts and underpants of the bathers. I would have as soon moved into Berenson's poolhouse as most of the residences I had seen so far in America.

"He's why they're here, of course."

"What?"

"The boys — they've come for Steve Rice. He's a real hero to that generation."

"Who are they, the boys?"

"The one with the ponytail is my nephew, Floyd. The others are friends of his — Jason and Jay, the blond bombshells. They think they'll make it in the movies, but really I've told them, this town is full of studs. The only way they'll make it is on their stomachs. Floyd now, he's brighter. He's coming back to New York with me, to learn the business."

"The accountancy business?"

Huey hung up his jacket, and took off his peach-colored silk shirt. He was lean and tanned, like every other man I had seen in California. My sense of physical inadequacy deepened.

"I work for Berenson International, Dave — which is the family concern. All this wealth was created by Berenson senior, as I'm sure you know — and when the old man died the problem was keeping it together, since his only son did not care for corporate politics. Or for anything else to do with his father. Well, we managed. We have an executive committee now running things and I have something to do with that."

Huey had stripped off completely, and was testing the temperature of the shower water with his foot.

"What does he care for?"

"Huh?" He lowered the volume of the water, and half turned to me.

"What does J.P. care for?"

"Oh, well —" He shrugged. "At the moment, Carol."

He stepped under the water, then out; began to cover himself with lavender soap.

"Is there any hope?"

"I doubt it."

He continued to soap himself for a moment, then moved back under the shower and stood, head tilted, eyes closed, as the water cascaded over his body.

"She's seen every specialist there is. Some say one thing, some another. There's talk of a shock cure, but I don't know. It's a gamble."

I turned away and looked through the plate-glass window. Howard was at the pool now, talking to Joey. There was no sign of Steve. Jason and Jay were prancing around, showing off, doing handstands and pushing each other into the water. Floyd appeared to have fallen asleep beneath an umbrella.

"There's one thing I don't understand."

"Only one?"

Huey had one of those disconcerting smiles which totally transforms an appearance: his made him abruptly handsome, yet dangerous at the same time — how could an accountant have such a smile?

"They say Carol was beaten up and raped one night, after hitchhiking in a canyon?"

"Right."

Huey shut off the taps, and stepped out of the shower.

"Well, what on earth was she doing there, all alone?"

"Ah, yes —"

He picked up a blue towel and began to dry himself.

"That's the one thing we're not sure about."

26

Berenson reached the head of the Palladian
staircase and turned right.

He hurried along a corridor lined with paintings by the
French Impressionists, then through a doorway leading to
the twentieth-century wing of the castle. There he paused.
The false urbanity with which he had greeted my news had
vanished. This was the face of a man in pain, hesitating
miserably outside his daughter's room. He listened intently
for a moment.

There was no sound.

He carefully tried the handle, turned it and slipped into
Carol's suite, then froze in the narrow hallway, staring towards an open doorway at the end.

She was there, standing in her bedroom, beside a triangular
high-school banner in yellow and black. A pitiful sight, this
shattered teenager amid the debris of her youth — the shelves
of yearbooks; the framed photos of Carol as a cheerleader
(in short skirt, knee socks, sneakers, and sweater in high-
school colors), arms cheerfully entwined with other girls'.
Swimming photos, tennis photos, graduation photos. Carol
in the black hat, the long black gown. By the bed, a tennis
racket, a Bjorn Borg poster, a TV set — (vision on, with no
sound; an early Judy Garland movie: *Meet Me in St. Louis*).
On the bed, a Snoopy dog.

Carol was standing before a full-length mirror in her loose
pale dress — to which she had added a silver Hermès scarf.

She twisted the scarf, entwined it in her long fingers, turned from side to side, never taking her eyes from the mirror.

Berenson watched from the hallway — his expression anguished. He wiped the sweat from his upper lip, and moved into a shadow as Carol turned to her closet. She returned to the mirror wearing — as well as the scarf — a crocodile bag, slung at a jaunty angle over one shoulder. She stroked the bag, adjusted its position, appeared calmed by it. A shaft of sunlight struck the golden *C*, which gleamed and flickered.

Then she moved towards a tall arched window and gazed out across the pine trees of the estate. Beside her hung a framed photograph of her entire class in graduation year.

Carol frowned, as at some distant memory.

Berenson moved away then — the rage building inside him. When he could stand it no longer, he left as silently as he had arrived.

27

On reading back what I have written so far, I feel that I have given a very sketchy picture of John Paul Berenson. The reason is that, for the sake of the narrative, I am relating these events in the order in which they actually occurred — rather than in the haphazard sequence I learned of them; and at this particular point in the story I knew hardly anything about him. If I were writing a novel, instead of simply putting down such facts as I know, I suppose I would now set about integrating the following pages into the mainstream of the plot; threading them into carefully selected scenes, using whatever craftsmanship came to hand. But the truth is less malleable than fiction, and the truth is that I had no chance during that convulsive weekend, nor in the stunned days which followed, to acquire even this meager information: and to contrive it otherwise would be to cheat on both the reader and myself.

It was not until much later — until everything was over and all our lives were changed — that I had the time and the opportunity to study the background of this remarkable man. Not that it was easy even then, even though everyone was cooperating to an almost embarrassing degree: such a complex structure of secrecy, forged over decades, could hardly be dismantled overnight — the mere fact that by the end J.P. wanted me to know everything was not in itself sufficient.

The passion for secrecy had begun with Berenson senior, the robber baron who hid his women and his thoughts, and who paid people monthly cheques for life simply not to reveal what they had done for him. (Many of these recipients are still alive and, since the cheques continue, still silent.) He wanted to own and keep from others the facts of his life, and he succeeded to a large extent. Bonds of loyalty, contractual restrictions and fear of reprisals further protected his privacy — and continued to do so, even after his death in 1959.

So I have still been unable to form any clear picture of how the old man built the empire. That he was equally at home with heads of state, waterfront bosses, bankers, governors and Mafia dons emerged clearly enough during the antitrust hearings of the forties; there was also much speculation about his two homicidal bodyguards, whose early schooling had been in the Cleveland mob; but precisely how this austere, patrician-looking immigrant, arriving penniless on Staten Island in the 1890s, had succeeded in entwining his fortunes with those of the government on so many levels, federal, state and local, remains a mystery.

Berenson International began as a loosely affiliated group of aviation and insurance companies, and mushroomed spectacularly between the wars with the benefit of an unprecedented series of federal contracts, licenses, franchises and subsidies. These illegal favors (maintain his enemies) continued to flow even after his death — with no direct involvement from his son. The uninterrupted access to public funds went on as if by magic, as did the compensatory cash payments to politicians and state officials; and while it is true that J.P. did nothing to strengthen these bonds, he did nothing to weaken them either; as such they seem good for many more years (and administrations) — like ivy on an old wall.

In fairness, I should add that these grave charges have never been proven, and it could be that I am doing the family an injustice by repeating them here. But I doubt it. The corrupt nature of the conglomerate is taken for granted by even the most generous-minded observers — the only query, which I share, being the degree to which J.P. was conscious of it;

all I do know is that he was aware — frighteningly aware — that he could take whatever he wanted from this world and be answerable to no man in return. That was why the business with Rosalind hit him so hard, and the business with Carol — these, as far as I have been able to discover, being the only occasions in his life when J.P. felt out of control of events.

Information about his wife is almost as hard to come by as facts about the family fortune. I know that she was English, and had been a fashion model in the London of the fifties — a Tory London of *Les Ambassadeurs*, The Dover Buttery, coffee-bars, the Princess Margaret set, the Milroy — which was where J.P. met her, after a first-night party for *The Boy Friend*. The war had been over for ten years, but J.P. still wore the aura of a hero. He had dropped out of Yale, enlisted at nineteen, sought out a combat assignment in the Pacific and, after being wounded, emerged as a decorated veteran in 1945. It was then that he gave the first of his two newspaper interviews (the second being upon becoming sole stockholder in the family concern). I have studied both, and found them equally unrevealing. One of several characteristics he shared with Steve Rice was an ability to talk to the media at length without actually saying anything.

He seems to have pursued the gentle Rosalind with the same single-mindedness he later brought to bear on her daughter: overwhelming her with a violent combination of sexuality and wealth. They were married in London in 1956. The next twelve years (punctuated by the birth of Carol in 1959) were spent closeted in one or other of his various homes around the world and, unexpectedly, in the compilation of an enormous biography of Coleridge, whose fragmentary, indefinable works had always fascinated J.P., and whose "Kubla Khan" was never far from his bedside. (I have read J.P.'s book, which was privately printed in Germany in 1965, but without illumination; I found it willfully contradictory and obscure — adjectives one could equally well apply to both the author and his subject, come to think of it, so perhaps I missed the point.)

After twelve years Rosalind finally gathered the courage to leave. She had been unhappy for some time, the regimented privilege of her life weighing more and more heavily as the deadly mid-thirties approached. Escape seemed the only hope, and in the spring of 1968 came her emotional dash for freedom. Berenson was shattered, and I have never been able to decide whether those characteristics — the aloofness of temperament, the air of secrecy and loneliness, the inability to unbend in the easy spontaneity and exchange of confidence that brings people together — were the cause or the result of that trauma. He certainly did everything in his very considerable power to get her back, but without success: she was one of those women who, slow to move, are intractable once the step is taken. She returned to London and sat impenetrably in the Oliver Messel suite at the Dorchester throughout his hurricane of grief. Neither threats, bribes, pleas nor the withholding of Carol had any effect on her. Eventually he had to face the fact that she had ceased to care for him, and that nothing he could do would ever make her care for him again. He faced it, but he could not understand it. Who could have anticipated it? He had taken her for granted for so long — how could he imagine that she would transform herself, at a stroke, from a familiar household possession to the most unattainable object on earth — the lost love: the one that got away?

He returned to California, and it was then that the *L.A. Times* began recording his solo trips into the desert: reporters in jeeps tailing his air-conditioned Lincoln Continental as far as they dared into the wilderness, until discouraged by unidentified sniper fire from the mysterious dunes beyond. The austere manner deepened, the self-control ossified around him — and when, twelve months later, Rosalind died, he betrayed no emotion whatsoever — flying to London for the funeral, speaking to no one, and flying out again the same day. (Her death is as shrouded in mystery as everything else. The official verdict was a heart attack after a late-night party. The unofficial ones are as various as you may imagine.)

But if his manner remained enigmatic, certain actions were not: that was the year the twelfth-century Cistercian chapel appeared in the grounds of Avonhurst, having lain crated up in San Francisco since 1958 — a forgotten caprice of Berenson senior's last trip to Europe. It was also the year he moved Carol squarely into the center of his life — forgoing for her sake any other emotional relationship (a situation which was to continue for almost ten years).

From then on he lived for her — his unpredictable daughter whose looks came from her mother and whose attitudes to life came from him: a combustible mixture. He watched her grow from deep, hawklike eyes: eyes which told of private sorrows which would stay private forever, even if every cent of his fortune was used to protect them.

And there my research ended, apart from the occasional fact — such as one I picked up from his chauffeur, Ace. About the same time, J.P. began collecting icons and reading the lives of the saints. On reflection, I am not at all surprised that his mind should turn in a religious direction — certainly he had no hesitation whatever in playing God himself, when the time came.

28

As Steve walked into the Renaissance refectory a few paces behind Kathy, I noticed that he had changed for lunch; he had on a silver vinyl shirt, cord jeans and moccasins. He was looking even more preoccupied than usual, and I wondered if he had already popped a third pill that day. Kathy had also changed, into her Indian cotton outfit; no makeup, no jewelry.

They crossed the vast room to the thirty-foot dining table and, as they reached it, everyone rose. J.P. introduced Huey, Floyd, Jason and Jay — all now dressed in tennis clothes — and we sat down again; ten of us perched on upholstered chairs with carved woodwork, under medieval Sienese banners.

A sudden sound made me turn; through a stained-glass window I saw three audio contractors, festooned in cables, tramping about the lawn, setting up a quadrophonic system for the party. They went on to test every speaker in turn throughout the lunch, thereby adding an electronic dimension to decor that fairly screamed for Vivaldi.

I looked around the table, thinking how neatly our status was defined by the seating plan. J.P. sat at the head of the table, with Kathy — the only girl — on his right. Huey was on his left, then Steve, then Jason and me. Steve was thus boxed in by admirers, especially as he had Floyd and Jay opposite. Howard was sitting next to Kathy, and Joey was across from me, at the end.

I was not feeling at all hungry. A combination of the heat

and the events of the morning had depressed whatever appetite I might have had; also my old sensation had returned — the one where I move several feet outside my body and hang suspended, staring down at myself and everyone else; not that it mattered much where I hung, since none of them apart from Joey (no conversationalist) had the slightest interest in talking to me. They were all far too concerned with their sexual priorities of the moment. (And this being California, priorities were all — no one had time for inessentials.)

The table could have comfortably seated twenty-five, so we were strung out with yards between. This, combined with the discordant blasts of rock (like the soundtrack of a Japanese film) made it hard to hear what anyone said, let alone join in. Not that I wanted to: from my suspended position I could see well enough what they were all up to.

Huey and the boys were working on Steve: they talked to each other across him and around him, but always for his benefit — to involve him. I do not think either Jason or Jay took their eyes off him once throughout the meal except when they were actually lifting food to their mouths — and not always then: at one point Jason dropped a large spoonful of raspberry mousse into the crotch of his lilac tennis shorts. From the occasional comment it seemed that music memories were being invoked — the Stones at Madison Square Garden, violence on the Led Zeppelin tour, the death of Elvis Presley — anything in fact which they thought might provoke Steve into some kind of personalized response (to borrow a phrase from Howard).

Floyd somehow had the idea that Steve was interested in Gothicism, so he kept talking about the Pre-Raphaelites, and ghosts and falconry and the transference of souls; but he might as well have saved his breath. Steve was not there — tranquil smiles and the occasional nod were the most anyone could expect.

At the remote head of the table, J.P. and Kathy were locked

[93]

into a conversation in which smiles and glances mattered more than words. Afterwards she claimed that they had discussed art at Avonhurst, and I am sure they did — but their real dialogue was elsewhere, as was obvious to all. I watched as one watches TV with the sound off: Kathy, quick, expressive, full of laughter; J.P. leaning forwards, that Aztec face relaxing, quizzical, intent. They might have been totally alone in some restaurant by the beach; and it struck me that J.P., as he talked to Kathy, looked about ten years younger.

I turned away from that — averted my mind from it — and concentrated on Howard instead. He looked even gloomier than I did; irritated and jealous in about equal proportions. Having twice failed to interrupt J.P., he had now taken to tilting his chair and calling past everyone's back along the length of the table to Joey — some technical jargon about the afternoon shooting session they had planned; but since Joey was only picking up about one word in three, he soon gave up and slumped forwards in his chair, elbows on the table.

At last the food arrived. Half a dozen dark servants in white jackets materialized, bearing wine, bread, bowls of salad, six kinds of dressing — and an enormous silver platter, cleverly balanced by the headwaiter, who appeared to have only one arm, which struck me as odd. Behind them, a short-haired woman in a linen uniform darted from the kitchen and across to the arched doorway, carrying a tray of food. I correctly assumed her to be Carol's nurse.

A terrific clatter beside me was topped by an electronic shriek from the lawn; a waiter retrieved his serving spoon from the mosaic floor, apologizing profusely in Spanish. I was beginning to develop a headache.

There was a lull in the conversation as the platter was set in the middle of the table. I could hear the hum of the air conditioning. Then the lid was ceremoniously raised, revealing a gigantic Pacific fish, served in the French manner, complete with head and tail: the mouth gaped, the needle teeth glistened, the dead-eye stared up.

I looked at Joey, who shrugged and grinned. I really was not feeling at all well.

29

A red tent unfolded like a giant rose between the pool and the shimmering green of the pine forest.

The electronics system had finally been regulated, and when we came out into the warm, scented air the only sounds were the tapping of tent pegs, the hiss of the water sprinklers, and a wave of insect noise.

J.P. came out first, talking closely with Huey, an arm thrown around his shoulders; both men were smoking large cigars. I followed with Steve — limp with relief that the surreal lunch was over. Howard appeared, announced that he had to run through the evening's PR procedure with Kathy, and disappeared again. Floyd, Jason and Jay, pulsing with energy, suggested we join them for tennis — which was quite a joke. I explained that I had a headache, while Steve simply shook his golden hair; so they enlisted Joey, and all four walked off across the lawn towards the poolhouse. Huey blew a cloud of smoke towards the sky, glanced at his watch and said he had to call New York, he would see us all later.

Berenson, relaxed and affable, turned to Steve. "What a poor host I am, Mr. Rice! I've hardly spoken a word to my guest of honor." He looked at me. "Would you excuse us?"

"Of course."

"You should lie out in the sun for a while," J.P. advised me. "You're kind of pale."

"I'll go and change," I replied.

He turned back to Steve. "Let's walk."

I watched them set off in the direction I had taken earlier —

towards the unicorn clearing. I was getting used to being left alone, but I did not mind. I would take an aspirin and lie down for half an hour, then change into some shorts and watch my British legs turn pink. I might even have a swim.

As I went indoors I tried to imagine what J.P. would have to say to Steve. When I found out later I was again amazed at the extent to which he knew us all.

30

Beyond the luminous clearing the vegetation thickened. The path wound between trees, conifers of some kind, spruce or fir. The light dimmed to a heavy green, punctuated by enormous blooms of white and yellow.

Steve paused, considering the camellias. "Everythin' grows, eh?"

"You just add water," replied J.P. "It's called 'Instant Paradise.'"

They walked on, past wild, unexpected juxtapositions of Asian and European flora.

"You can plant an African date-palm next to a Swedish elm — everything flourishes. Like the Garden of Eden."

"Complete with rattlesnakes." Steve grinned. "Our slide guitarist got bitten in the ass by one last year."

A shallow stream swirled between smooth stones towards the artificial lake. An old oak had been thrown across, with a handrail formed of a branch of ash.

"Howard tells me you're a nature lover. That's interesting."

"If you're born in Brixton you've got to be. I hardly saw a tree 'til I was thirteen."

Berenson led the way across the narrow bridge. "I also read a lot about your tour. Howard sent the clippings."

"He's always working."

J.P. smiled, and glanced at Steve with a certain appreciation. "I especially liked the story of the paraplegics."

"Eh?"

"In Denver?"

There was a pause. Steve had forgotten. J.P. prompted —
"Six of them waiting at the stage door, all paralyzed, hoping
you'd cure them —?"

"Oh yes, right. The laying on of 'ands."

"What I liked was the fact that you tried it."

"Well, why not? It's all in the mind. I'm as qualified to faith-
heal as the next idiot."

J.P. looked at him in silence. Then — "Did you actually
expect them to stand up and walk?"

"I don't know. I hear two of them are much better now."

J.P. continued to regard him. "I also wondered how it must
feel, to be so . . . idolized?"

"I never think about it."

"No? What do you think about?"

Steve paused. It was the first nonsocial question, complete
with overtones. It was also the one he had least trouble in
answering.

"Music," replied Steve, equably.

The foliage thinned out after the stream, presaging the
Oriental landscape ahead. Berenson led the way along a winding path which dipped suddenly, then rose to reveal a cherry
orchard in full bloom; beyond the orchard, in a circular clearing, stood a Japanese pavilion, glimmering in the heat.

Steve halted, staring at it — his head to one side, as before
a painting.

"This is where my daughter spends most of her time," said
J.P.

"Lucky girl."

Steve stood in the lush grass of the clearing, regarding the
ornamental, two-storied building. From an alcove above the
doorway, a statue of Kwan-on, Japanese goddess of mercy,
smiled serenely down upon him.

"We're going to Japan next month," said Steve. "Perhaps
I'll buy a pagoda! There's one in Kew, you know?"

"Kew?"

"In London — in the suburbs. I rented a flat there once, with my first money — or maybe it was Richmond. Anyway we all got kicked out for smoking dope and too much noise, so I used to write songs in Kew Gardens." Steve smiled, and shook his head. "And there was a Japanese pagoda. I always remember that."

J.P. watched thoughtfully as Steve walked around the building, past water sprinklers and a stone lantern.

"I'll show you the inside," he said.

31

The interior of the pavilion was Japanese
modern: low-slung rattan furniture, painted screens, opaque
blinds, shelves of Eastern and Western books bound in yellow
silk, iris plants, enormous cushions on the floor — and a TV
set embedded in one wall. The atmosphere was calm, and
somehow neutral — no photographs, no personal momentos.

Berenson came from the heat into the heavy, frigid air of
the interior, followed by Steve. It was dark at first, after the
brilliance of the clearing — the light filtering, blue and mystical, through slatted blinds across the bamboo-framed
windows.

Steve stood, looking around.

"Peaceful," he commented.

"It was originally called 'The Temple of Limpid Solitude.' "

J.P. sat down on a chiselled stool, inlaid with scenes depicting the gods of heaven and earth bathing in the river of
life.

"That's what I need," observed Steve. "Some limpid solitude."

Like almost every room at Avonhurst, the pavilion bulged
with treasures: ancient artifacts intricately carved from ivory
and jade — the least valuable of which could have supported
a man for years.

J.P. sat watching as Steve examined a startlingly erotic
statue of a temple dancer from Kyoto.

"It's ideal for my daughter, of course."

"What?"

"Tranquillity. It's the only medicine those doctors agreed on."

Steve put down the statuette, and studied a modern Japanese painting entitled *Osaka in the Rain.*

"Does she sleep here too?"

"No, she sleeps in the house, but she spends her days here. Very quietly. Or in the orchard. Trees have a calming effect on her." He paused. "Trees and television."

"I really like this painting," said Steve. "D'you want to sell it?"

"No."

"It reminds me a bit of Dufy."

"It's a little like a Dufy."

"Listen, I'm really sorry about your daughter. What 'appened? A car crash, or something?"

"Not exactly."

There was a brief silence.

"As a matter of fact, I'd like you to meet her. Would you agree to that?"

"Why not?"

J.P. rose, crossed to the book shelves and pulled an ornamental rope. A bell sounded faintly.

"You mean she's here?"

"She is nearby. She's not expecting to see you — she hasn't been prepared in any way. I just think it might be interesting — for us all."

"Sure." Steve smiled.

He turned again to the canvas: misty clouds over a river, a street full of tiny cars, pedestrians hurrying. "I wanted to be an artist, you know? I was going to study painting if the music thing hadn't worked out. I 'ad my name down for three different art schools."

Behind him, a shoji screen slid silently back; Carol's nurse appeared, then hesitated.

Carol emerged from behind her, pale and fragile. She gazed, without expression, at J.P. — who had moved to the window — then at Steve, who still regarded the canvas.

"This is my daughter," said J.P.

"Ah, yes —" Steve turned, brightly —

"How do you do?"

"How do you do?"

He crossed to Carol in the dim light, hand outstretched, a smile on his face.

She stood rock still, staring at him. J.P. pulled a cord: the blind slid up, flooding the delicate room with light.

Steve blinked inquiringly towards him, then looked at Carol. He could see her properly now. Her tragic face. His smile faded. He lowered his hand. His expression changed from puzzlement to concern in the space of a moment.

She was staring at him with a mute intensity such as he had never seen. He was familiar enough with adoration, but he had never before seen such terrible, silent pleading. He did not know what it meant, or what to do. He could not take his eyes from hers. He stood there, feeling helpless and idiotic, for what seemed like minutes instead of seconds.

Finally he stepped back and turned to J.P. for guidance. None was forthcoming. J.P.'s eyes were riveted on his daughter: as if her reactions at this moment were all that mattered in the world.

Carol made a pitiable gesture, like some lost, broken child, and began to tremble. Silent tears ran down her hollow cheeks. Steve could bear it no more —

"Listen —" he said urgently to J.P. "I think I'd better go."

The trembling redoubled. She was shaking uncontrollably now. The nurse hurried from the doorway, took her by the shoulders — but Carol would not budge. She sank to her knees before Steve, her body quaking, shivering; a deep choking came from her throat, as though she were trying to articulate in the silence.

The nurse squatted beside her; soothed her; looked at J.P., who still made no move.

"I should've warned you." Steve crossed to the door. "I 'ave a weird effect on some people, when they first meet me."

J.P. looked at him then — a long, strange stare.

"I'm sorry." Steve shrugged sadly. "One of the paraplegics fainted on the spot." He looked at Carol, then back at J.P. "I'll be at the pool, all right?"

He slid open the door of the pavilion and hurried away into the heat of the clearing.

J.P. gazed after him for a moment, closed the door and stood, head bowed, deep in thought. Carol's fit began to subside; the nurse held some kind of sedative inhaler under her nose and coaxed her to her feet.

J.P. straightened himself. Unclenched his hands. Made his decision.

He crossed the room to a red lacquered door beside the Osaka painting; took some keys from his trouser pocket, unlocked the door and pulled it open, revealing a deep, dark cupboard. He switched on the interior light.

There — hanging from the clothes rail — was a military-style U.S. canvas duffel bag.

J.P. stared at the duffel bag; reached in and shifted it an inch or two along the rail. He gave it a push so that it swayed gently back and forth before him.

32

A silver-striped dune buggy bowled merrily down the twisting drive and skidded to a halt in the gravel courtyard at Avonhurst.

In a giggling flurry of legs, sandals, beach bags and cameras, two teenaged girls clambered out and ran towards the archway. I saw them just as I was crossing to the pool, and almost dropped my London newspapers. They really were pretty: they had long, streaked hair, one fair, one dark; deeply tanned, endless legs beneath Ginger Rogers tap-dancing shorts; sunglasses pushed up on top of their heads and pink T-shirts with *Let's Get It On* stencilled across the front. They headed for the poolhouse without noticing me and then, hearing voices, veered off to the tennis courts. They called out "Hi!" to the players and stood there for a moment, arm in arm, considering them. Joey had been about to serve when they first appeared, and was so moved as to put the ball straight into the bottom of the net. Jay, Jason and Floyd seemed less affected — merely returning the hi and concentrating on their game.

I continued on to the pool, still looking at them. I was extremely pleased that these girls had arrived; they were just what we needed, I thought — and just what I had always heard L.A. was about. Golden teenagers, the California dream of eternal youth in the sun. They did not stay long at the court. Having distracted poor Joey into a series of double faults (to the thinly disguised contempt of his partner, Floyd), they walked away, calling cheerfully, "Have a nice game!" Neither Jason nor Jay gave them a second glance as they disappeared into the poolhouse.

I settled myself on a chaise beside the water, put down my newspaper and towel, removed my British-army-surplus shirt, adjusted my swimming trunks, removed the top of a tube of Nivea sun cream and began to apply it to my chest — reflecting as I did so on the boring amount of normally unconsidered skin that has to be taken into account on such occasions.

I sat there, squeezing the tube and rubbing away while an army of caterers marched to and from the red tent by the pine forest; crates of champagne were arriving, glasses, trays, oranges and lemons; buffet tables were being erected, and colored lights set in the trees; it was going to be quite a party. I thought about the girls again. J.P. had said something about the superintendent's daughters wanting to meet Steve, so maybe that was who they were. I imagined they must be now stripping off in the poolhouse, and held that thought for a minute. I hoped they would soon appear in their bikinis and plunge into the water. I was in dire need of distraction.

Then the cause of all my tensions emerged from the castle and crossed the lawn towards me — Kathy, with Howard striding beside her. He carried an important-looking folder, and his expression was grim. The day was getting away from Howard, I felt. He had been in a bad mood ever since Steve took that stand on the heavies. (Perhaps he really was concerned about security?) The news of the Hillcrest killing appeared to have thrown him too, and being semi-ignored throughout lunch had not helped. The fact was that Howard — for all his superconfident life-style, his Lear jet, his mansion in Brentwood, his full-time butler — had one of those egos that need daily massaging if it is not to wilt, and no one at Avonhurst had paid any attention at all. (Nor would they tonight, I reflected — with Berenson as host and Steve as star, Howard would again be relegated to the background.) On the other hand, he was producing the album and the film; he was making a great deal of money and I did not feel too much inclined to pity him; furthermore, it was possible that I had the whole thing wrong — after all, Howard might be just as scared of losing Kathy as I was myself. One thing was sure, however: whatever the cause of his dissatisfaction, some of it was about to be vented on me, the most vulnerable employee in the pecking order — cuckolded husband or not.

"Take a good rest now, Dave," he called, when they reached the pool. "You're going to need it."

I raised myself on one elbow, inquiringly. Howard picked up a wicker stool, plonked it down and sat beside me. Kathy perched on the diving board.

"Twenty minutes maximum," she smiled at me, referring to my sunbathing limit, at least on the first day.

"Here's your copy of the guest list," said Howard, handing me a bunch of mimeographed sheets, stapled together. "Study it. You're going to meet every one of them tonight."

"I am?" I considered the list.

"You're looking at a hundred of the biggest music-names in America. Producers, arrangers, singers, disc jockeys. Now, in an ideal world I could simply film them at the party and incorporate that into our movie. But these self-important schmucks say no — invasion of privacy! Their idea of fun'd be to pitch the cameras into the pool, and the operators with them."

A certain bitterness in his tone reminded me that Howard had begun his career as a photographer — had been one, in fact, until his recent association with J.P.

"How about when Steve meets Stephanie?" I asked.

"Oh, listen —" his voice rose. "We're filming that all right.

Joey's set up for it, and so are the Lookalike people. That's different. That's a milestone, for Christ's sake. That'll make rock history! Even these cunts will see that."

Howard picked up a discarded beach towel and wiped some sweat from his face.

"Where do I come in?"

"Well Dave, your job is just to listen." He leaned over the pool and plunged both hands into the water. "Because I plan to outfox them! Reconstruct this party next week. Restage the whole fucking thing here, on this lawn, using actors or even extras — it's just a crowd scene, for Christ's sake. What do you think?"

I hesitated. It was a terrible idea.

"Well," I began.

"But I'll need dialogue. All the bitchy cracks that float around this pool tonight!"

He was staring at me now, looking half demented, in my opinion.

"Especially the ones about me — there'll be plenty of those! So hear and remember — but don't make notes or you'll end up with your head busted in the bushes."

He sighed, flicked some more sweat off.

"Can you manage that, Dave?"

"Why not?" I replied. "Graham Greene says all writers are spies."

"Sure." Howard rose heavily.

"I mean, I wish to God I could simply bug the place, put mikes in the trees," he sighed again. "So — stick by me. I'll introduce you as they arrive, then point you at the best action."

"And the best girls?" smiled Kathy.

"There'll be plenty of those." He picked up his folder. "Where's Joey?"

"Playing tennis."

"OK then, Dave —" He clapped me on the shoulder with

[108]

a kind of paranoid heartiness. "You won't let me down." He walked away towards the courts.

I looked after him for a moment. "There goes a worried man."

Kathy groaned in agreement.

"And yet he was so dominant this morning," I could not resist adding.

"It's first-night nerves. Howard's not cut out for the big time."

"Or maybe he can't take being ignored?"

"What?"

"Like all through lunch?"

"I didn't ignore him — I was just talking to the host." She looked at me. "Are you going to give me a hard time for that?"

I reached for the sun cream without replying.

"He's an extraordinary man, the host. You should talk to him yourself."

"I have."

She watched me rub cream into my legs for a moment, then shook her head. "Honestly! This morning you were going to leave me because of Howard, and now you're upset that I ignored him at lunch. Try to be logical, honey?"

"This is not a logical day."

"But try, hm? We should help each other. We could be the only sane people here."

"Including the host?"

"Maybe. I haven't figured him out yet."

"But you will?"

"I'd like to. I mean, how often do you meet a man like that? He's so — unexpected. What did you talk about?"

"English women."

"He was married to one."

"From Wiltshire, like the castle."

"Isn't that amazing?" She concentrated; frowned slightly, focusing her thoughts. "But he confuses me. Scares me, too. There's something almost . . . mystical about him. Howard says his whole life is dominated by love."

"Love?"

"For his daughter. I haven't even met her, but can you imagine? That poor shattered creature who can't even speak and yet she rules him? Everything he does is for her. He won't leave her, not even for a day. That's why he never travels. He only thinks of her. How to cure her."

I remembered what Huey had said, and it was there again: the fear.

"Did he say that?"

"He hardly mentioned her. Howard said that."

A pause.

"What else did Howard say?"

"Oh, a lot about Berenson senior. That monster! He's behind it all, I'm sure."

"Behind all what?"

"Our host's frozen manner, for one thing. It's just a defense. He was terrified to show his emotions as a kid, and he still can't. Except to Carol — which is probably why he loves her so much."

I thought about that. It made sense.

"Why doesn't he run the family business?" I asked.

Kathy shrugged. "Howard says he's spent half his life trying not to be like his father. And his big regret is that he didn't have the guts to give it all away and start from nothing."

"Well, he didn't," I said.

"No, he didn't."

Kathy hunched forwards, restively. "But Howard remembers the old man — says he was the coldest thing on earth. He had no love in him at all. He used to tell his son: 'People are governed by the head. A kind heart is of little value in chess.' "

"That's sort of true."

"If you see life as a chess game!" Kathy snorted. "And if you're prepared to treat your only child with contempt, and ignore it and humiliate it —"

"He did all that?"

"Apparently. He was disappointed with the boy. Found him weak and inadequate and unworthy of the succession."

She suddenly sat straighter on the diving board, self-consciously.

"It's pretty extreme, isn't it?"

"Well, this is California baby," I said, deliberately flip. "Where only the extremes are normal."

She looked at me for a moment, then stood up. "You're full of shit today."

Kathy glanced across the lawn to where Joey, having been extricated from the doubles, was now being lectured on the grass by Howard.

"Have we got any Valium?" I asked.

"In the bedroom. By the bed. I'm going to talk to Joey."

I nodded, glumly.

"And I think Howard's got a point. You need a rest." She walked away.

I sunk back onto the chaise. I considered going indoors for the tranquillizers, but decided to save them for later, in case things got worse. I closed my eyes and concentrated on emptying my mind of all trivialities — but it did not work (it never does), so I opened them again and watched two butterflies chasing each other around a white umbrella.

Then I saw Steve slouching across the lawn from the direction of the unicorn clearing. I waved and he came over and sat down on the stool vacated by Howard.

That was when he told me of his experiences with J.P.

33

The girls emerged from the poolhouse and spotted Steve immediately. I really thought they were going to pass out. They stopped in their tracks, gawped, stared at each other, swallowed, and sat down right where they were, on the verandah.

Steve did not notice them. He had removed the vinyl shirt and the moccasins, and was lying beside me on his stomach, staring down into the water.

I was still trying to rationalize it all: the implications of his confrontation with Carol Berenson.

"So she cried," I said. "What else?"

"She made noises. Terrible grunting noises, as if she was trying to talk."

"Well, perhaps she was. It must be awful not being able to."

"But it was all at me, you know? At me personally — as if I had some kind of answer."

"Well, maybe you have."

"I don't even know the question."

I studied him for a moment. "Are you sure you've never met her before?"

"Who could forget? Even I couldn't forget that face." He shook his head. "She's probably seen me on film, or something." He raised himself abruptly on one arm. "Or else she's just nuts."

He picked up the silver shirt, opened the breast pocket and took out his enamel box. "Is there anything in that bottle?"

I passed the Perrier water.

"How many's that today?" I asked.

"Three. D'you want one?"

I shook my head. Steve tipped the bottle, swallowed the pill, drew several deep breaths, snapped the box shut. He returned it to the shirt pocket, then rolled over onto his stomach again and looked downwards.

I followed his gaze:

Steve's reflection shimmered mysteriously up at us from the deep spectrum of the pool. The image rippled gently, in and out of synch with the dancing rhythms of the water.

"He's weird too — Berenson I mean. Didn't say a word. Just stood there staring, while she went ape. Didn't say a bleeding word!"

"What could he say? The nurse was there —"

"He could've helped me out. I was doing 'im a favor, for Christ's sake."

He continued to stare at the reflection.

By this time the girls had found the courage to approach us; they came padding along the side of the pool, and I noticed that each one was carrying a copy of the *Self-Made Man* album. They looked every bit as good as I had anticipated — a little better, if anything, honey-brown in their white bikinis. The blonde spoke first.

"Hi!" She smiled, revealing expensive California dentistry. "I'm Susie, and this is my sister Kate."

"Welcome," I said. "To wherever this is."

We all shook hands.

"I'm Dave, and this is Steve."

They perched on the edge of my chaise, gazing at him. Steve made the smallest conceivable movement.

"Hullo," he said.

"Hi!" they replied, together.

Then he turned his head away, resting it on his arms. Susie and Kate were both breathing audibly.

"Are you the superintendent's daughters?" I asked.

"Don't hold it against us?"

"He's a tolerant cop!"

"One of the best."

"He needs to be, with us around!"

They both giggled and glanced sideways at Steve.

"I mean, he never busts people."

"He only deals with homicides — so unless you've killed someone, don't worry."

"Also he's a real good friend of Mr. Berenson's. That's why we're here."

"Daddy knew the father, too, years ago. Berenson senior."

"He came to a party here once, for Humphrey Bogart. How about that?"

"Terrific," I said.

Kate turned, and added solemnly, "I think a party for Steve Rice is even more terrific."

I waited for Steve to acknowledge this, but the third pill appeared to have sent him to sleep.

"He's a bit quiet today," I explained.

"Oh listen, I can relate to that."

"Why should he talk?"

"He says everything, just being there."

"He exists — what else matters?"

"His songs have said it anyhow."

They paused, and gazed at Steve's back.

"Does he meditate much?" asked Kate.

I supposed that this was as good a description of Steve's mental processes as any.

"Sometimes."

"I told you," said Susie to Kate. "It's the only way."

"I'm studying yoga myself," said Kate.

"Now she thinks her navel is the center of the universe," giggled Susie.

"Well, why not?" I considered Kate's rounded stomach. "It's a very nice navel."

[114]

"I guess you're British too, huh?"

"Why's that?"

"You all have this crazy sense of humor."

I was just about to expound on the meaning and significance of British humor when there was a tremendous splash, followed by a drenching shower of warm water.

We all turned in time to see Floyd surface.

"Hi, everyone!" he said, then hunched into a professional crawl which ploughed him along the pool to a few feet from Steve's face.

The splash had aroused Steve, and Floyd's spluttering emergence made him sit up quickly; he blinked, pale and alarmed, towards the poolhouse.

Jason and Jay — jockstraps bulging, torsos oiled and gleaming — raced each other into the water. Jason executed a perfect belly-flop, while Jay hit the surface ass-first, knees tucked under his chin. Between them they soaked pretty well the entire poolside area. Floyd shouted with laughter, and turned —

"Hey, Steve!" he yelled, treading water. "We just thought of something. How about rock as a war substitute, huh?"

Steve sat up on his heels for a moment, looked at me, then considered the three swimmers as if they were so many insects in the pool.

"Can you see where I'm coming from, Steve? I mean, given that it releases so much aggression and all —" Floyd unclipped his ponytail, held his nose, ducked his head under water and reappeared, straightening his hair. "And given that violence is the norm of our society — maybe rock's a harmless outlet, huh? Like football or something? What d'you say?"

Steve regarded him for a moment longer, then stood up.

"You could be right," he replied.

He pulled the Eliot paperback from the hip pocket of his jeans and moved off to a chaise several yards back from the pool. Floyd looked after him, wonderingly.

"Wow," he exclaimed. Then he turned over and back-crawled past Jason and Jay.

"I could be right, fellows."

They all laughed: but it was not pleasant laughter. There was no humor in it. It was beginning to look as if Steve had been ruder than I had realized at lunch, and that Huey's boys were feeling snubbed — which was a pity, especially if they truly admired Steve; on the other hand they were boorish and unsubtle to a degree and deserved whatever they got, I thought. The trouble was that it made for an unpleasant atmosphere.

The telephone beside the pool rang. Everyone looked surprised. It rang again, then stopped by itself.

There was a silence.

I glanced across at Steve. He had opened his copy of *Collected Poems*. The hummingbird was back, hovering just to the left of his head. My stomach contracted again: the day's alarm was still building, and I still did not know why.

I considered Jason, who had clambered up onto Jay's shoulders. He hurled himself into space and landed flat on his back in the middle of the pool: the biggest splash of all, gaining further applause. I looked at the girls, who had followed these antics without expression.

"What a bunch of assholes," remarked Susie.

"Steve'll go soon," predicted Kate. "Let's get his autograph." She picked up a *Self-Made Man* LP.

"Will he sign this?" she asked me.

"I have a better idea," said Susie.

She reached behind, unfastened the top of her bikini, and stood up.

"Oh yes," I settled back. "That's a much better idea."

Susie took a yellow felt-tipped pen from her beach bag, said "Come on," and crossed to Steve, carrying her bikini top. Kate followed.

"We're sorry to disturb you." Susie kneeled beside him. "But would you autograph this?"

Steve lowered the *Collected Poems* and looked at her — the eager face, the golden breasts. He smiled, accepting her pen and the narrow strip of white fabric, which he rested on his knee.

"And we apologize for those creeps," she added, as he inscribed his name.

"They're not your fault."

"They're our nationality."

"They're on some kind of macho trip, I think," said Kate. Steve handed the bikini top to Susie.

"It'll never be washed," she told him.

"Do you read much Eliot?" breathed Kate.

Steve nodded.

"I think he's incredible," she said. " 'April is the cruellest month, breeding/Lilacs out of the dead land, mixing/Memory and desire, stirring/Dull roots with spring rain.' Wow! *The Waste Land.* I think he's the most meaningful poet of the twentieth century."

"Do you want me to sign your bra too?" inquired Steve.

"Oh, right — thanks." Kate fumbled with her bikini top. There was a slight pause, as the clasp was twisted. She had my full attention.

"There —"

She got it off and handed it over. Her breasts were larger and higher than Susie's. She patted her long dark hair as Steve signed the inside of the left cup.

"But to me Eliot was kind of a visionary. A kind of a man who could live by visions — d'you know what I'm saying? Like folks in olden days who had the knack, and we've lost it. That's what I think. But we need it. That's why so many kids are on dope. We need the visions. We have dreams, OK — but they're not enough. I don't think so."

Steve paused, interested — the white bra in his hand.

"She really gets off on Eliot," explained Susie.

Jason raised himself halfway out of the pool and shouted: "Why don't you have him sign your pants too?"

"That's for later," said Jay.

They all laughed.

"Hi, Huey!" called Floyd.

I turned, and there was Huey — heading briskly towards us across the lawn.

Susie and Kate stood up.

Huey waved to me, nodded to the girls, and then squatted on his heels beside Steve.

"A message from the host. He'd like to show you some film."

Steve regarded him blankly. "What film?"

"That's what he'd like to show you. You'll enjoy it, Steve."

"I'm enjoying the sun too."

"It'll only take a minute."

"I'll see it later."

"He's screening it now."

There was a pause. I felt sure Steve would refuse. Then Huey smiled that disturbing smile of his —

"And he wants to apologize for the drama just now. He hopes you won't hold that against him?"

Steve shrugged.

"He also says this is the last favor he'll ever ask of you."

Steve rose, slammed down the *Collected Poems*. "Anything for some peace," he said. He picked up his silver shirt and walked off towards the castle.

Huey called to the athletes, "Let's go, boys."

They obediently hauled themselves out of the pool, adjusted their jockstraps, smoothed their hair, and gathered up their towels.

"I'm told you've seen this film, Dave." Huey smiled at me. "So I'll leave you in charge of the girls."

He hurried away before I could reply. I sat watching Steve cross the lawn, followed by the four of them.

A servant appeared on the terrace, leading the two German shepherds on chain leashes. One of the dogs snarled at Jason, and he turned aggressively — as if about to kick it in the face. He thought better of it however, and they all disappeared into the castle. The servant walked away with the dogs, towards the courtyard.

All was suddenly quiet by the pool; the water settled back into its flickering patterns; the girls settled back onto their air mattresses, autographed tops tucked safely into beach bags; Howard, Joey and Kathy murmured together on the grass thirty yards away. I relaxed on my chaise, gazed up at the perfect sky, and wondered what J.P. could possibly want to screen that I had already seen? Something of Howard's presumably, but then Steve would have seen that too: it did not make sense. Furthermore, I could not shake the impression that I had been deliberately excluded — Huey had been altogether too bland, in too much of a hurry. So why should they not want me? On the other hand, why should they? Nothing added up today. It was one of those days.

I rubbed some more cream into my stomach and reflected that here I was, beside a swimming pool in the company of two topless nymphs, one of whom (Kate) I found particularly disturbing. The activist in me demanded some kind of move; the animal in me was not unstirred either; sexually speaking, the tour had been a washout. Kathy had been either too tired or too busy (or just plain disinterested) since our first night in New York — so I had been celibate for six weeks, which for me was a record. Not that there had not been opportunities: Steve's every move led us down paths lined with panting, conniving girls, most of whom would do anything, literally anything, to get near him. The spin-offs for his entourage were endless: the backup group and crew had been exhausted since Chicago. However, I had remained faithful throughout — hoping thereby to tell Kathy something, to make some point I had never bothered about before in nine careless years. My well-deserved reward was that she had not even noticed — yet even so I persevered, turned away, passed them up in a dozen cities across the States. It was beginning to look as if I could only deceive my wife when sure of her love: a worrying thought.

I shifted a little and studied the girls. They were lying flat on their backs, eyes closed, knees raised, arms relaxed at their sides, faces tilted reverentially towards the sun. It was clear enough that, from my Olympian position at their idol's right hand — and given the contemporary state of sexual mores in California — I could probably have the pair of them, if I so chose. And why not? My current tactics were getting me nowhere. Always change a losing game, as the great Bill Tilden used to teach his juniors.

"Have you known him long?" Kate's dreamy voice interrupted my thoughts.

"About six months."

"He looks so gentle, huh?" remarked Susie, her eyes still closed.

"He looks like he'd take forever."

"Great ass, too."

They both sighed, and changed positions on their mattresses. I stood up, crossed to the chaise Steve had occupied, and picked up his copy of *Collected Poems*.

"They say he hardly knows which town he's in," said Susie. "I read that in *Rolling Stone*. His memory's gone."

"An angel has no memory," replied Kate.

The Eliot paperback fell open at "Burnt Norton." There was a passage marked in pencil —

> *Go, go, go, said the bird: human kind*
> *Cannot bear very much reality.*
> *Time past and time future*

What might have been and what has been
Point to one end, which is always present.

I read it again.

The servant with the German shepherds recrossed the lawn, heading towards the unicorn clearing; the dogs strained heavily on their leashes.

Huey's phrase reverberated in my head: "This is the last favor he'll ever ask of you." There was something I did not like about that.

I looked across at the south terrace: the afternoon sun on it had a quiet and menacing stillness. I shut the Eliot decisively. I had to find out what was happening to Steve.

34

He was sitting on a wide pullman seat in the suede-lined screening room, smiling in the flickering light. Huey had been right, Steve was enjoying the show: himself — performing his own hit number "Self-Made Man."

The song was almost over when I opened the chrome-and-leather door at the rear of the screening room and slipped, silent and unobserved, into the back row. I blinked around, adjusting my eyes to the darkness. Huey was beside Steve, sunk right down, chin in hand, one foot resting on the seat before him. Berenson sat nearer to the screen, and away to one side. He was half turned — watching both the film and Steve's reaction to it. The boys were scattered around the auditorium, huddled in their towels against the freezing air conditioning.

I sat motionless, inconspicuous — and more confused than ever. They were watching the conclusion of last year's concert at the Amphitheater. We had screened the opening for the press that morning, as an introduction to Howard's *Steve Rice in L.A.* film. Why should the finale be so interesting to J.P.?

As the famous song ended, Steve's arms fell from the guitar, and he stood still for a moment, eyes closed, face raised to the spotlight. Then, as the sea of applause broke around him, swelling and roaring, he bowed his head and stepped backwards from the microphone.

A line of Hell's Angels blocked the front of the stage as the shouting and cheering built and the camera focused on the audience: row after row of applauding, worshipping fans.

Like most filmmakers, Howard had selected certain faces to favor, and for a while he was intercutting between a master shot of the Amphitheater and a series of enormous closeups of individual spectators: some fainting, some weeping, some simply gazing at the stage as if God himself stood before them.

It was not until the camera held for the third time on a particular face in the front row that Steve sat a little straighter in his seat.

"I know that girl," he remarked.

J.P. moved his left hand and touched a button on the armrest beside him. The image of the girl froze on the screen; the sound cut off; we were left staring at an enormous, grainy closeup.

I frowned in the silence; I knew her too — I had met her somewhere, no doubt of it. But how could I forget anyone so pretty? Still nobody spoke. I fancied I could hear them breathing.

"Is that what you wanted to show me?" inquired Steve. "That girl?"

"We want to fill in a few gaps, Steve." Berenson's voice was quieter than I had ever heard it — hardly above a whisper.

"What gaps?"

J.P. turned fully around to face him. I sank a little further into my seat.

"After the concert that night, there was a big party, do you remember?"

"Was there?"

Steve thought. The recollective process was truly agonizing for him.

"Given by a man named Milton Rubin."

"Oh, yes." Steve sounded dismissive. "At Malibu."

"Exactly."

"It was awful. Is that where I met her?"

"That's where you met her." J.P. paused, then continued, expressionless. "And later on you left with her."

"I did?"

Steve looked dubious; then concentrated fiercely again; after a moment his brow cleared. "Hey, you could be right! Someone did get me out of there that night."

"Get you out?"

"I was in bad shape. Really. I had some stuff to take me through the concert, and then they were all leaning on me — the guest of honor, you know? In the end I went into the bathroom and climbed out of the window." He stared at the screen again. "And she was outside, that's right!" He nodded several times. "She offered to drive me along the beach in her new car, with the top down." He paused. "Who is she, anyhow?"

J.P. was silent. Huey replied for him: "Just someone who's disappeared, Steve. We're trying to locate her."

There was a pause, and that was the moment I almost cried out: I had got it at last. I had seen that eager, passionate face not two hours before, ruined and helpless, beside a cypress tree. It was Carol Berenson.

J.P. stood up, and flicked on the houselights.

"But you didn't drive along the beach, did you?"

"Didn't we?"

"Do you remember being in the car at all?" asked Huey.

"Oh yes — for the getaway. It was funny. I had to keep my head down. We were laughing a lot."

Huey and the boys were all around him now. Steve had a great audience.

Images formed in his mind:

Carol, semi-drunk at the wheel, reversing aggressively in the narrow driveway of the Malibu house, braking, leaning across, half out of her white dress as she shoved open the fat door of the Ferrari —

Steve running from the oleander bushes, bent double, crouching over the gravel. His boots and long bejeaned legs swinging in as Carol shifted her crocodile bag and adjusted

[124]

the silver scarf around her neck. Both of them shaking with laughter as he slammed the door shut and she revved the big engine — "Get down!" she hissed, looking towards the beach where Howard was taking flash photos of guests against the moonlit Pacific. Carol engaged the gear. She lowered the window and yelled, "Still grafting, Howard?" as Steve slid almost to the floor and Howard turned startled in time to see the car roar out of the driveway.

J.P.'s eyes had never left Steve — eyes which seemed to look beyond what they saw. "And then?"

Steve shrugged. "She put the top down and drove."

"To Coldwater Canyon?"

"Christ, who knows? It was a year ago. Besides, I was 'allucinating by then. I think I even passed out at one point. Except —"

He paused; they all waited.

"I do remember 'aving a swim that night, so we must have gone by the sea, mustn't we?" He shrugged again. "Anyhow, I flew to London at the crack of dawn. I know that because it was the first time I ever slept all the way home."

Steve stood up and stretched. "Let's get back to the sun, hm?"

That was my cue to leave, while he still had their attention. Keeping my knees bent, and my head hunched into my shoulders, I shuffled sideways — the quickest and quietest sidestep in the world — across to the door and out.

35

I did not go back to the sunshine because I could not face them yet: I had to think. I hurried up the Palladian staircase to our room, which was on the second floor overlooking the courtyard.

I rummaged around the bed for Kathy's Valium, poured out some Perrier, and swallowed a ten-milligram. After that I collapsed onto the four-poster, stared up at the embroidered canopy, and tried to work out what to do.

The fact was that Steve had just freely confessed (with no idea of the implications) not only to having met Miss Berenson before, but to having gone for a drive with her on the night of a party one year ago. Whether that had also been the night of the assault, I did not know — but supposing it had? That would account for Carol's breakdown when confronted by Steve in the Japanese pavilion: if her wounded mind associated him with the violence of the canyon. Of course, nothing so far began to explain why she should have been alone there at two A.M. — but there were enough links now to suggest that Steve might have the answer to that, too.

In which case why had they not asked him? Prodded his memory? Honestly faced him with the situation? Not only had they not done that: they had even concealed the real identity of the girl on the screen. Once they saw that there was no connection in his pill-soaked head, they had made no effort at all to enlighten him.

I brooded long over this, but could find no explanation; and the more I thought, the creepier it became. My generalized anxieties of the day now focused on Steve: something was going to happen to him, I felt sure. I had no idea what, or if it could (or even should) be avoided. I only knew that, to be fair, someone ought to plant in his bemused brain the idea that the girl in the front row had not been just another fan at his concert, sitting beside some glamorous people, including a fairly well known TV actor: she had been his host's beloved daughter.

My course of action was therefore clear — find Steve, take him aside, and tell him; and if only I had done it there and then (as I have thought a thousand times since) everything might have ended differently. But it is in my nature to delay — to let life slide by while I lie around on beds planning how to live it. In this particular instance, what I did was to reach out, switch on the radio, and lie there for a fatal ten minutes listening to a local news bulletin (fires in the mountains, earth tremors in San Francisco, the heat not expected to break for days).

The sound of a car starting in the courtyard recalled me to my purpose. I leaped off the bed, went to the window and looked down. Everyone appeared to be leaving. Howard sat, revving up the Jaguar; Susie and Kate slid in beside him. Floyd, Jason and Jay helped Joey heave his filmic equipment — camera, lights, tape recorder, cables — into the VW bus. While I watched, Steve hurried through the archway and joined them.

I turned from the window; if I ran down I might catch them. I threw open the bedroom door and found myself face to face with Huey. He was still dressed in tennis clothes, and was carrying three rackets.

"I've come up to get you," he smiled, moving into the room. "They're all off filming, so I thought you and I might play a set together."

I looked at him; I felt certain that he had stayed behind to keep an eye on me.

The VW bus started up with a clatter. Huey crossed to the window and looked out. "There they go. Nice view you have from here." He turned back into the room.

"Where's Kathy?" I asked.

"She's gone for a walk with J.P. She's fascinated by the estate, because she comes from Wiltshire herself. Isn't that a remarkable coincidence?"

I sat down heavily on the bed.

"Did you bring your own racket, or would you like one of these?"

He offered me a shiny metal Wilson. I accepted it, held it in my hand, stared at the strings.

"That should be about your weight."

I nodded; I had never before in my life felt so totally futile.

"I'm looking forward to this." Huey smiled encouragingly. "Howard tells me you have a tremendous backhand."

36

When the party began at eight o'clock, Steve had still not returned, and there had still been no chance to speak to him.

The sun was low over the Pacific and the last rays were slanting into our room as I emerged lobster-pink from the shower, a huge blister on my right thumb, another on my left heel, sweat-soaked tennis clothes in a heap on the floor. Cars were being valet-parked in the courtyard below as I dried myself in a yellow towelling robe, poured talcum powder over my feet and climbed into my party outfit: the vertical-striped blue shirt which Kathy said made me look thinner, white trousers which I always thought were too tight, and my often-repaired Gucci shoes. I combed my hair, which was still wet, picked up the Robt. Burns cigars and the Ma Maison matches, and hurried out of the room.

Howard caught me at the foot of the Palladian staircase.

"Where the fuck's Kathy?" he demanded.

"I was going to ask you that."

It was a fairly brisk reply, and it made him pause.

"Well, I just got back, Dave." He modified his tone. "We found a great location out by the Spanish chapel." He looked at me for a moment, then clapped me on the shoulder. "Come on, let's have a drink."

We crossed the hall, our heels clicking on the North African marble floor.

"You got some sun, huh?"

"Did you really tell Huey I have a tremendous backhand?"

"Sure."

"Do you know that Huey once took three games off Lew Hoad?"

We emerged onto the south terrace, where the caterers had set up one of their various bars; it had a genuine brass rail and appeared to be stocked with every brand of liquor in the world.

"A pretty sight," observed Howard.

He stood considering the bottles with the air of a man determined to sample them all that night, and I knew the feeling; I felt fairly inclined to join him.

"Let's start with champagne."

A waiter materialized with a bottle, which he opened and left in an ice bucket beside us. I looked towards the mountains; they had turned violet blue in the strange light the sun made now, deepening and softening all the colors. A flight of birds crossed the pale sky, then vanished against rose-flecked clouds to the west. Howard turned to me —

"While I have you to myself I want to tell you how much I've appreciated everything."

"What?"

"You're an honest man, Dave — and you've been a tower of strength on the tour. You could have gotten angry many times, especially with me — I knew that. But you never did. You kept your head and your dignity — I admire that. I admire it very much."

Oh God — I thought — he is going to get serious.

"Think nothing of it."

"But I do. I do."

He was staring at me again with the same intensity he had shown by the pool. I sipped the Dom Perignon.

"Great champagne," I said.

Really, I thought, I must stop him before he plunges into some embarrassing confession about Kathy; they claim to have eliminated guilt in California, but they have made a

[130]

pretty poor job of it in my opinion; and as far as I am concerned, it is bad enough to be cuckolded without having to be told about it as well.

"You're so British, aren't you? Hiding everything you feel. But I know how sensitive you are. You have one skin-layer less than the rest of us."

"I will have tonight, anyhow." I raised my sunburned arm, but he did not smile.

"You keep it all inside, don't you? You really suffer in silence. Well, maybe you're right. Maybe that's the way to be. I should learn from you. We have more in common than you realize."

"Let's drink to that."

"We might as well — you obviously won't talk about it." He picked up his glass, and studied me. Then he added: "Just so long as you know that I know, and that I'm grateful and I understand and sympathize with you and your problems — right?"

"Right."

We both drank, and there was a silence. It had been a close thing. I changed the subject.

"What do you think of the Kellerman girls?"

"They're kids." He shrugged.

"Is that bad?"

"I guess I'm not old enough for them. I still like grown-up women. I need the dialogue, you know? And the challenge. I mean, Kate and Susie, what are they? Interchangeable."

"Well," I said. "I'll interchange them with you anytime."

Howard laughed briefly, then stood gazing out at the last of the sun. "I'm going to help you all I can now, Dave. I know you've had it bad — professionally speaking."

"How do you know that?"

"From Kathy. She talks about you all the time."

"Oh, great."

"She cares for you. She told me how you won a prize for

your first play, and then wrote all those 1960s themes before anyone else."

"She told you that?"

"And how other people lifted them and got into production first. She says you're the best writer in England, and everyone else has gotten rich from your ideas."

"Kathy exaggerates."

"So you're not talented?"

"It's better to be lucky." I shrugged.

"Well, perhaps now you will be. And if you're good as well, that's better — then you'll be ready for the luck."

"I've always been too bloody careful," I said. "Too bloody cautious." I emptied my second glass of champagne. "I overprepare, you see? I take too bloody long, so all the hustlers get in first."

"Then stick with me, kid. It takes one to know the others. We'll galvanize you out here. L.A. could be the place."

"Could it? This joke town? No serious writers live here, do they?"

"Serious writers? That's something else. What's a serious writer, anyhow?"

I paused. I could have answered him easily the year before. I probably still could if I tried — but I did not much want to. I refilled my glass.

"But as for Kathy," he added, "I just think as long as she's on the payroll she ought to be around. Don't you agree?"

"She went for a walk with Mister Berenson three hours ago."

He turned to me, started to say something, changed his mind. I raised my third glass: "To absent friends."

"What a fuck-up," he muttered.

"Oh, I don't know. Just because you have no host, no secretary and no star —"

"Steve's back."

"Ah." I took a large swallow. "I must talk to him."

[132]

"He'll be down."

The first guests were being ushered through the bougain-villea-covered archway; J.P.'s thick-set majordomo pointed them in our direction. I saw a plump, unhealthy-looking man, flanked by two girls of unearthly beauty, advancing towards us among the shadows of the pine trees across the lawn.

"Hiya Howard," the man called. "This is some place, huh?"

"Milton Rubin," murmured Howard. "Wouldn't you know he'd be first? And the girls are dikes. Come on, into battle."

As I followed him down onto the lawn I thought how much better I liked Howard now all that superconfidence had gone.

I also decided that the things which alarmed me at Avon-hurst were probably nothing to do with him at all: the chances were that Howard knew no more about them than I did myself.

37

By the time Steve made his entrance there were a hundred people in the garden, the mountains had turned gray and the first stars were out.

The technicolor crowd surged across the lawn, swelling with new arrivals, dissolving and re-forming as guests were presented to each other and moved on; the air crackled with the sound of show-business folk greeting each other as if the three-minute warning had just gone — their voices pitched a key higher than the Jamaican reggae group which had been flown in from New York to provide live background music throughout the night.

I stood on the verandah of the poolhouse clutching my fifth glass of champagne, watching waiters weave in and out of the throng and trying to suppress the feeling that it could not be real. I had already been introduced to marketing men, publicists, entrepreneurs, arrangers, record-company bosses, agents, concert promoters, disc jockeys, actors, songwriters, managers, television MCs, impresarios, record producers and more girls than I could ever get around to; I had met them all, as Howard had promised. A large number had asked me to repeat my surname, then to spell it — after which they had lost interest; but a few had stayed on, suspecting that I might be some obscure-but-important cog in the wheel of the Berenson empire.

I stared off to the southeast, where the distant architecture of downtown Los Angeles was beginning to glow in the dark — the boulevards, the jewelled sky-signs, the great light-show; then back to the verandah, where girls and men in silks and suntans disappeared and reappeared before me in the warm dusk, discussing (in a language that seemed to contain fewer words than the Eskimos') themselves, each other, and their endless affairs. At first I had tried to do right by Howard, to register these conversations and store them for the future, but I was not having much success — partly because I was getting drunk, but mostly because of the sheer banality of the material. The occasional comment on Berenson stood out: "But he's the son of his father," said a huge man with a hair transplant. "He inherited a mob, so what do you want?" When I inquired as to what this might mean, he winked heavily and began to discuss cosmetic surgery.

I kept a dutiful ear open for jokes against Howard, but did not hear any — just the occasional wisecrack about Carol ("probably locked up in the West Wing, like Jane Eyre"). In the end I decided, out of my newfound respect for Howard (and with all due respect to reality) that I could invent more amusing dialogue than this in my sleep, and who would be the wiser? Thus comforted, I abandoned the effort.

After a while I noticed that the Jamaicans were not playing anymore; conversation had dropped, and there was a general buzz of anticipation; someone gave vent to a wild, uncontrollable giggle as J.P.'s majordomo, now magnificent in hunting-pink, strode onto the terrace, raised both hands and bellowed:

"Ladies and gennelmen, Steve Rice!"

To a burst of applause, Steve came through the carved doorway. He was dressed entirely in white and looked very handsome. He had washed his hair — which must have accounted for the delay — and he stood alone for a moment, arms held out slightly from his sides, regarding the eager crowd; then he smiled and waved, and from the relaxed way he did it I knew he had taken a fourth pill that day. (I waved back, but he did not see me.) Kate and Susie emerged behind him — glowing brown in their halter dresses of pink and white respectively — followed by Jason, Jay, Floyd and Joey, all flushed, bathed and expectant; the six of them escorted Steve down to the lawn, where Howard was waiting.

I decided that this was not the moment to take Steve aside — besides, I needed another drink first. I plucked one from a passing tray and reflected, as the Jamaicans began to play again, that the presence of Joey in the group was a reassuring factor. Nothing terrible could happen with good old Joey around.

The crowd had shifted after Steve's arrival, spilling away towards the buffet tent; I found myself next to a skinny black superstar dressed in an I. Magnin herdsman's caftan, a rope tied headband, a stack of bracelets on one wrist and a red-and-blue Cartier watch on the other. She had been talking for some time.

"So the studio is costing me money, more importantly the whole thing is costing time, I'm telling you that if I'm at a recording studio at three in the morning I want to have something for it. I told them, I said, listen, I don't have time to screw around. I said it like that so they'd understand what I was saying."

Her principal audience — a middle-aged lady with an enormous hairdo who was drinking vodka gimlets and holding a rolled-up copy of the *Hollywood Reporter,* and a small man with tangled gray hair and a bushy beard — both nodded deeply.

"*Quo vadis,* baby?" said the man.

"I love your watch!" cried the hairdo, bending over the superstar's wrist.

"I have another one the same, only it's green, with a black face."

The superstar looked at me and smiled. "Who are you?"

I gave the question so much thought that she had turned

away before I replied. "I'm Howard Vance's own personalized playwright."

"*Quo vadis*, baby?" said the bearded man, who was wearing a tiny silver coke spoon on his necklace.

Everyone smiled. People smiled a lot in California, I had noticed, but hardly anyone laughed. They smiled because they had all heard about humor and because they had great teeth and they spent fortunes on their dentists — but genuine laughter seemed rare. I thought maybe it was considered bad for the face, and just as I was about to inquire, I saw something which cleared everything else out of my mind:

J.P. Berenson standing under the bougainvillea-covered archway with Kathy.

I stood staring at them, wondering why on earth they should appear from that direction, rather than from the castle? Either they were being very discreet, or else they really had been for a walk. On the other hand, Kathy had on her red dress (the one she usually considered too much), so she had obviously been back to our room since I came down. When I started towards them she saw me at once, said something to J.P., then turned to me; she looked lovely.

"There you are!" she said. "Did you find the Valium?"

"I found them."

"Don't drink too much, hm? How many did you take?"

"Not enough."

Kathy was looking at the guests. "So many people!"

"I don't know how you've managed it," I went on, "but you've got mascara on your mouth."

"Oh look, there's Howard."

She gave me a quick kiss on the cheek, then joined the throng. I stood watching her and the red of her dress as it merged with the turquoise and scarlet and saffron and gold on the lawn.

I turned to find Berenson beside me.

[137]

"It's good to see the place full again," he remarked.

I looked at him directly. "Is it?"

"A home like this should be always full. I've been too long between drinks."

He shook his head, lost in some private reverie; I felt an irresistible desire to shake him out of it.

"I was in your screening room today," I said. "Sitting at the back. I saw the whole thing."

He turned his gaze towards me then, considering me with his curious eyes; he nodded.

"Huey thought you were there." He took my arm. "Let's walk a little."

38

We skirted the crowd and crossed the soft
grass to the tennis courts. J.P. paused beside a white-blooming
oleander and lit a cigar; his face — by the steady flame of his
match — was as inscrutable as ever.

"The girl on the screen was Carol," he said, "as of course
you realized."

"But Steve didn't."

"That's irrelevant. He knew he was with her that night, so
at least we have the right man."

J.P. extinguished the match.

"And now what?"

He flicked the match away into the darkness.

"Now nothing."

"Well," I said, "I don't believe you. Shall I tell you what I
think? I think all this business, this inviting Steve down here
and everything — I think it's all part of some plan you have
to do with Carol. Some idea you have for curing her —"

"Oh yes," he interrupted tiredly. "Why should I deny it?"

I paused.

"It was our last hope, you see? The shock cure. To reconfront her with the actual man she'd been with, to dredge up
all the fear and the panic of that night, in the hope that —
after so much time — her conscious mind might somehow . . . deal with it."

He studied his cigar in silence.

"But it didn't work. Oh, she felt the fear all right. She
trembled like an animal at the sight of him. But since then

[139]

there's been nothing. I've spent the last few hours with her — she's hardly moved, or looked at me."

He paused, controlling himself with an effort.

"We have exorcised nothing."

At that moment I suddenly understood what Kathy had meant by his "mystical" quality: there was something truly elemental about the man — he was like some primal source of power and suffering and loss. It was impossible to disbelieve him.

"And why the screening?"

"To double-check. To be sure we'd found the right man, and that her fit was for the right reason. Of course, by then I hoped not! I hoped he wouldn't recognize her, and that after all we'd made a mistake. Because then there'd be someone else to look for, and there'd still be hope."

A roar of laughter from the pool area made me turn; someone shouted "You've got to be kidding!" several times. I looked back at J.P.

"How did you get on to Steve in the first place?"

"Through television." He shrugged "A news program the day you arrived in New York."

Then, while dinner guests drifted by towards the buffet tent, he told me of Carol's TV obsession, of how she had sat transfixed and silent for months on end before the colored screens in her high-school bedroom and the Japanese pavilion — impervious alike to visits from therapists, teachers, relatives, specialists and friends. She had neither spoken, read nor written a single word in the ten-and-a-half months since she had left Cedars and — in spite of repeated assurances to the contrary — J.P. had begun to feel all hope was gone, that she had been irrevocably wounded in some secret area of herself.

Next came Howard's breezy phone-call from New York: we had arrived, the tour was on, J.P. could see us all on TV at six o'clock that evening. When the news program began,

Carol was sitting on her bed, the Snoopy dog on her lap, gazing at the screen. J.P. was working in his study, having forgotten about the whole thing. The nurse was boiling water in the tiny kitchen next to Carol's room.

The cameras had picked us up as we emerged from Customs, and for the first few moments the screen was filled with images of Howard, surrounded by flamboyant members of the backup group and their assorted wives — all of whom had dressed as outrageously as possible in the hope of diverting the media from Steve (at least long enough for him to slip through unnoticed between Kathy, Joey and myself). In their transparent tops and split skirts the girls had almost made it when an enterprising *Washington Post* reporter recognized the back of Steve's head, darted around and blocked our maneuver. There was an immediate realignment of all eyes and cameras, and that was when the screaming began in Carol's room.

J.P. took the Palladian staircase at a run but, by the time he reached the top, Carol was already being sedated by the nurse. Steve's serene image shone beside her bed, fielding questions from half a dozen reporters at once. Berenson stared at Carol, then at the TV — while the nurse explained that, in her view, there was some connection between his daughter's outburst and the diffident, graceful creature on the screen. That night phone calls were made, the deductive process concluded, and plans to bring Steve Rice to Avonhurst were put in hand.

"We'd've been on to him before," said J.P., "if Howard hadn't been so sure she left the party alone."

"But I mean, what happened? How did they get separated?"

"We may never know. He can't remember and she can't tell us. But it doesn't matter now. It's over."

J.P.'s cigar had gone out; when he relit it the flame shook a little — though his face was as expressionless as before.

"I can't help her anymore. I must just accept that. I must

get back to my own life now." He turned me away from the tennis courts, towards the buffet tent. "I'd like to travel again. Perhaps write a little — about my father. Clear up some mis-understandings. Who knows how much time any of us has left?"

Howard saw us, and called, "Hey, John!"

J.P. turned to me with an air of solemn finality.

"I've told you this because I like you, Dave. You're an honest man and you deserve the truth." He held out his right hand, and I shook it. "If I can help at any time, in any way, let me know. And don't let my problems spoil your party. There are some good connections for you here."

As he walked off towards Howard, I reflected that this was the second reference to my honesty coupled with an offer of help within the hour; so either I was looking particularly genuine and helpless that night (which was depressing) or else Kathy had been talking again.

I saw Steve by the buffet tent, hemmed in by the usual status-conscious group. Huey, Floyd, Jason and Jay were standing nearby. I saw Kathy join Howard — but she looked straight into Berenson's eyes when she smiled. When Howard introduced some new arrivals, J.P. appeared to relax. His somber mood fell away; he smiled, expanded, took command of the group. Kathy murmured something and he laughed aloud.

Watching him, I suddenly felt this man had given up hope of nothing whatsoever: he simply was not the type.

39

One hour later a black Mercedes glided into the courtyard, the doors flew open, and a strange figure, cloaked and hooded, descended.

Two men who looked like business executives led this mysterious creature through the archway and across the lawn towards us.

Joey saw them coming, signalled to Howard, and then hurried away. Howard took Steve by the arm and led him up onto the raised verandah of the poolhouse. He beckoned to me, and I joined them there. The Jamaicans stopped playing in mid-number. One of them handed the microphone to Howard, while stage lights were switched on, flooding the verandah; when Joey returned with his movie camera he had to jostle for a position with several other cameramen who seemed to have materialized out of nowhere.

Howard tapped the microphone for silence, then cleared his throat.

"This will be a short speech, my friends," he said. "You all know we're here tonight, in this beautiful place, to celebrate the musical event of the year — the forthcoming release of Steve Rice's album *Reflections*."

Everyone clapped. Steve was looking at the hooded guest, who stood by the verandah — head bowed, face shadowed.

"I believe this to be his finest work to date, on a profound and contemporary theme. Twelve new songs which tell of how we mirror one another in this life, how we see ourselves reflected in each other's eyes — how the good and the bad in each of us is echoed in the rest. We are all one, that is the message of *Reflections* — one world, one spirit, one humanity."

Howard paused significantly, then flashed his boyish grin.

"I'm quoting the back of the album — but as I wrote it myself I guess that's fair!"

He paused again for the laughter, then continued:

"And now I want you to meet the face that will launch a million covers this fall — the face of Steve Rice himself, which he has never seen before tonight!"

Howard stepped back. There was an anticipatory drumroll from the Jamaicans, the movie cameras began to whirr.

The hooded figure stepped up onto the verandah, unfastened the clasp at her neck. The cloak fell to the ground revealing a Pre-Raphaelite girl who really might as well have been Steve's twin: a pale and graceful beauty with the same fragile, aesthetic features, the mane of blonde hair. They were even dressed alike, in white silk trousers and shirts, and although she was probably two inches shorter than Steve it was really only from her breasts and her fine slender hands that you could tell them apart.

There was a startled silence, then a burst of appreciative show-business applause. The girl bowed, and then turned to Steve. When she held out her hand to him a battery of cameras flashed, and when he took it the applause grew. The guests were impressed. I suppose that by daylight it would not have worked so well — but in the chiaroscuro of the verandah there was something almost supernatural about the resemblance.

"They're even the same age," called Howard. "Twenty-two years apiece!"

Steve shook his head bemusedly. From the transcendental state he had achieved that day, he seemed to be doubting the evidence of his senses. For a moment he thought that he was only dreaming her — or that he was somehow back amid the swirling pinks of the mythological looking-glasses, next to what he had called "the truest mirror on earth." An unknown girl was gazing at him with his eyes, smiling at him with his mouth. Even the hand she reached out to him was his hand, except it was slimmer and the nails were polished —

He did not believe she could be real, but when he touched her, when their fingers met and he felt their softness and their smooth warmth, he knew they were the real fingers of a real girl who looked exactly like him; and when she shook his hand for the photographers, her nails pressed lightly against his wrist, and he knew beyond doubt that he was not dreaming her; and when she stood next to him for the movie cameramen he could actually smell her — could inhale the fragrant, musky essence of her — and that was even more potent proof than the fingernails. I do not think Steve had ever been so moved by anything in his life before.

"Who are you?" he asked her.

"Well," she smiled, "my real name's Antonina, but they're calling me Stephanie for this."

"Who's calling you Stephanie?"

"The Lookalike people. The ones who found me. They have most everyone now. I mean, they have Jackie Onassis and Frank Sinatra and the Beatles. But if I have to look like someone, I'm real glad it's you."

"She's a talented kid, Steve," said Howard. "They found her in New York."

"I was playing second lead in an experimental drama about a deaf black boy," she told him. "The whole thing was kind of a visualization, you know? Of his psyche. But all in silence, kind of like a Magritte, do you know what I'm saying?"

Steve nodded — hypnotized.

"I used to sit motionless for an hour with a raven on my lap. It was incredible. They took most of the cast from a psychiatric ward."

"She's a talented kid, Steve," said Howard. "With or without the raven."

He gathered up the brown mantle Stephanie had worn for her entrance and draped it across her arm. "Remember, honey, when they start playing dance a little for the cameras, huh?"

He patted her ass, and muttered aside to me — "Don't let me down, eh Dave?"

He beamed at Steve, returned the microphone to the Jamaicans, and jumped down from the verandah.

Steve asked Stephanie, "Is that your cloak?"

"Yes?"

"Have you read *The Waste Land*?"

"Sure." She thought for a moment. "That'd make a movie too."

Steve turned to me abruptly. "Do me a favor, Dave? I've left my book in the VW bus."

"Right," I began. "But listen, I have to talk to you —"

"We'll talk later."

He returned to Stephanie.

She smiled at him. "You're looking at me kind of funny, Steve. Do you mind that we have the same face?"

"Mind?"

"Some do." She shrugged. "Some of the originals. They even tried to close down the agency once."

"Well, I don't mind."

"I guess they feel threatened somehow. In their identities. As if they're not unique anymore."

"Well, I don't feel that."

"What do you feel, Steve?"

The stage lights were extinguished, and she lowered her voice. "What do you actually get, huh? When you look at me?"

A musician plucked an experimental chord on his guitar.

Stephanie's eyes were huge and blue violet in the glow of the verandah. "What do you really think of me?"

"What do I think?" He studied her for another moment. "Shall I be honest?"

"Please."

He smiled. "I think you're beautiful."

When the Jamaicans began to play again, I left.

40

I passed under the bougainvillea archway and across the courtyard to the VW bus. I opened the back door, switched on the interior light, and rummaged around for Steve's book. I heard a murmur of voices behind me and turned.

J.P. was standing on the front steps of the castle, with Huey; they were both smoking cigars. Floyd, Jason and Jay came out of the castle and joined them. Floyd noticed me and waved. I waved back, and after a moment they all turned and went into the castle. I found the *Collected Poems* and — curious about the connection between Stephanie's cloak and *The Waste Land* — opened the volume and flicked through it. Since Steve always marked his favorite passages, I found the quote immediately:

> *There is always another one walking beside you*
> *Gliding wrapt in a brown mantle, hooded*
> *I do not know whether a man or a woman*
> *— But who is that on the other side of you?*

I switched off the interior light, shut the rear door of the VW, and returned to the party.

I walked up the stone steps of the south terrace, propped myself against the brass rail of the bar, and looked across the blue lawn towards the verandah. Many people were dancing now, and the noise level had risen. I picked out Kathy and

Howard, Kate and Joey, Susie and Milton Rubin. (His female escorts having taken up positions by the pool, at the feet of the black superstar.)

The dancers seemed to be drawn magnetically towards the middle of the floor — where the double image of Steve and Stephanie swayed and glittered, fused together in white and gold, impervious to all.

A loud cracking sound, followed by a thud, made everyone turn. A photographer had fallen out of a tree near the poolhouse. I watched as the man clambered to his feet, apparently unhurt, anxiously examining his camera. There were shouts of laughter, and ribald comments. The Jamaicans stopped playing; J.P.'s majordomo set off purposefully in that direction, and I supposed that all photographers would now be asked to leave.

I took advantage of the distraction to walk down the steps and across to the poolhouse. The dancers had separated and were moving around, talking and drinking. There was a faint-but-pleasant smell of hashish in the air. When I reached the verandah I found Steve and Stephanie still close together, just as the music had left them; when I approached them I honestly could not tell one from the other, so I addressed them both.

"Here's the book," I said.

"What book?"

Steve detached himself and turned to me, as if from a great distance, still keeping one arm around Stephanie.

"The one you asked for."

"Oh, great. Thanks Dave. Now we've got everything."

He reached out, but I held it firmly. "I have to talk to you."

"Talk?"

"It'll only take a minute."

I looked at Stephanie.

"I could go to the bathroom," she volunteered.

[149]

"I really must talk to you," I told Steve.

"I could go to the bathroom and powder your nose." She giggled, and kissed him.

Steve tightened his arm around her. "Look at that, Dave! Isn't she fantastic? Look at that face. What do you think? What a face . . . What is there to talk about?"

"Well," I said. "There's the screening."

"What screening?"

"Of the concert film, this afternoon —"

"Oh, Christ."

He bent and kissed Stephanie long and deep on the neck.

"They showed you a girl, remember?" I went on. "A blowup of a girl and you said you'd met her before?"

"Did I?"

"Listen Steve, it's important —"

"No, it's not." He straightened up and looked at me. "It's not important, and I'll tell you why — because I've never met a girl before. I met the first girl of my life tonight."

Stephanie pressed against him; she kissed his left ear, and then his eyes; when the Jamaicans began to play again, she swayed in time with the music, but he turned her away towards the pool. They were leaving.

"Here's the book," I said.

He took it and smiled at me. I stood alone on the verandah watching them walk past the lighted pool and off among the dark shadows on the lawn beyond. I did not know what else to do.

People began dancing all around me and I still stood there, wondering what else I could have done. Then I saw Kathy beside the pool, talking to a disc jockey. She was holding a silver album cover with the word *Reflections* embossed across it. I walked over to her and when I arrived she turned and pushed the album cover into my hand.

"Tell me what you think."

She went on talking to the disc jockey while I studied the

album cover. It was made of reflecting silver paper, and the idea was that, as you tilted it, you would see either a photograph of Steve alone, or Steve with Stephanie superimposed, or merely a reflection of your own face. Three possibilities, all according to the angle at which you held the cover; a brilliant piece of graphics, I thought. After a while, she turned. "What do you think?"

"Come for a walk." I handed the cover back to her.

She hesitated. "We're supposed to be working."

"Come on." I took her arm.

She glanced around, but there was no sign of Howard or J.P. Nor was there of Huey, Floyd or the brothers. The place seemed to have filled up with people I had never seen before.

"We could sit there," I said.

"All right."

We sat down on a chaise longue, just beyond the main glare of the pool lights. The waiters were still working well, and a tray of champagne appeared at once. We each took a glass, and Kathy gulped hers rather quickly. She was still looking around nervously; it was as though she was running some enormous risk by being there with me. I glanced down at my own glass, and found that it was already empty. I called for another.

"It's been a great success," Kathy said. "Howard needn't have worried."

"No one should ever worry," I said.

The waiter came hurrying back with the tray of drinks; I helped myself to two glasses plus a third for Kathy, and as I passed her the champagne I saw that she was looking at me with that sad tenderness I dreaded. She bore the unmistakable air of a woman who has reached a decision she knows will hurt you and which she had not intended to tell you just yet. Well, I was in no particular hurry to hear it either.

"Except about Steve," I continued. "Everyone should worry about him."

"Why?"

"Because he was with Carol Berenson the night she was attacked."

Kathy was still looking at me, but her expression had changed from fond regret to a kind of startled deadpan.

"I've been trying to tell him for hours, because he doesn't realize it. They all do — J.P. and Huey and the others — but he doesn't. He's forgotten, and he couldn't even recognize her because she's changed so much. I don't think Howard knows either, but I'm not sure."

I drank some more champagne. Kathy cleared her throat and said in an absolutely neutral tone, "Why should that matter?"

The question surprised me.

"Because whoever left her alone that night is totally responsible for her condition."

"But he didn't rape her, or beat her up —"

"He caused it to happen. Those truck drivers, or whatever they were — they were just animals, passing by."

"Why would Steve leave her there?"

I shrugged. "Maybe he forgot her."

"Well," she said, "I don't believe it."

"But you believe he was with her?"

"So I've been told."

"Ah." I paused. "By J.P.?"

"Yes."

I felt the now-familiar lurch in the stomach, and drank some more champagne.

"How very forthright of him."

"He had no need to, either. I mean, I had no idea."

"Why didn't he tell Steve?"

"Why should he? Why embarrass Steve and spoil the weekend? It's over anyway."

"Is it?"

"It's all over. He just wanted them to meet in case it might

[152]

help. So he could feel he'd done everything he could for her, and now he has. Everything in the world for that poor girl, and now it's over."

I sat there, looking at her. "And does he still confuse you, our host?"

"Not so much." She smiled.

"I had a feeling he didn't. I had a feeling you'd figured him out by now."

"He's a good man, Dave."

"Well," I said, "Howard and I thought you were probably figuring him out all the afternoon."

"We talked a lot."

"But did you actually figure him out Kathy? Because if you did that's the fastest you've ever figured anyone out since I've known you. You usually take more time."

She looked away, across the pool. "Do you want to hear about it?"

"Not really." I set down my empty glass. "But Howard might. He wonders why you never figure him out anymore." I rose unsteadily to my feet. "He says we have more in common than I realize — but he's wrong about that."

"Listen, Dave —"

"I realize everything."

And with that I walked away. I did not even wait for her answer and it was the first time in my life I had ever done that, ever turned my back on Kathy and walked away. If there had been a door, I would probably have slammed it. I simply could not look at her anymore or trust myself to speak; my fears for Steve and my crumbling marriage seemed suddenly fused in this single confidence of J.P.'s — that he could tell her something he had so well concealed from Steve himself. How could he trust her so? (Or did he merely think she would hear it from me anyway?) I gave up. I felt drunk and exhausted from the day's emotions — and from the unease that had settled on me the first moment I had seen that ravaged

[153]

figure by the cypress tree. I have never felt myself to be particularly psychic or even superstitious, but I now had the strong sensation of going through something that had all happened before. Whatever would be at Avonhurst, would be. There was no help for anything in life, I decided.

I crossed the lawn obliquely, among the guests star-scattered on the grass — trying to remember Omar Khayyám's lines about empty glasses. Howard stepped off the dance floor with Susie and called out to me:

" 'Strangers in the Night!' "

I waved to Howard, not understanding.

"Steve and Stephanie," he called happily. " 'Strangers in the Night!' " He mimed a man playing a violin.

I waved again, and walked on. I thought Howard was probably going to figure Susie out quite soon. After a while I collapsed rather heavily under a pine tree and closed my eyes. I heard a rapping sound in the branches above me. I looked up and there was a paper lantern hanging there and several jungle-sized insects were trying to commit suicide by ripping it apart.

A burst of applause from the direction of the verandah made me turn; the black superstar had accepted the microphone from Howard and was about to sing. I leaned back and breathed deeply. The air smelled of gardenias. I closed my eyes again, but did not enjoy the sensation, so I opened them and stared at the tall trees to the east of the castle. The landscape was unstable unless I concentrated on some fixed point.

That was when I saw Carol Berenson's nurse emerge from the darkness of the trees and hurry up the stone steps of the south terrace.

I wondered why she should be doing that so late at night, and then I closed my eyes again.

41

I woke up when the black superstar began to sing.

In Steve's honor she had chosen the most lyrical track from the *Self-Made Man* album: a love lament steeped in loss and quiet perceptions, which she performed with such truth and artistry and depth of feeling that I for one could not have begrudged her a dozen multicolored Cartier watches for each skinny arm and leg.

The guests fell silent, and the terrace filled up with Mexican servants who came out from the castle and stood listening, their hands clasped respectfully before them. I shook my head to clear it, lit up a cigar and blew smoke at the sky while the million-dollar voice throbbed through the warm night, telling of things which should be but are not, which could be but never will —

And Steve heard it too.

He was walking with Stephanie along a curving path between scented hedges. Their heads were close, their arms about each other, and at first he thought he was only imagining the song — dreaming it in his mind the way he had on the day he first composed it. But when Stephanie stopped to listen too, and then looked at him with a strange mixture of awe and passion he knew that it was being sung for him, and he was happy.

He led her past the scarlet unicorn — shining dark in the

moonlight — and then along the only path he knew at Avonhurst, towards the Japanese pavilion.

They had slipped away from the party with everyone's connivance and approval, of course. I could understand Howard's elation: a real relationship between Steve and his double would mean a publicity bonanza of unparalleled proportions. He was prepared to fake one anyway for the media — but a genuine, public affair between the total look-alikes on the *Reflections* album cover was a news item to be valued in millions.

That was why no one followed them and no one tried to interfere in any way as they wandered hand in hand, pale and golden through the grounds of Avonhurst — like mythical twins in a fairy tale. The castle became a feudal silhouette against the sky behind them as they moved between tall trees drained of color by the moonlight, past camellia bushes with their huge, white blooms, and on towards the stream. The frogs were full of life that night and there was the sound of the stream bubbling between the stones, and the sound within these sounds was the achingly beautiful voice of the black superstar — and as they crossed the oak bridge and walked on along the winding path, neither Steve nor Stephanie felt any need for words.

The path dipped, turned, and then rose suddenly to reveal the cherry orchard, the blossoms shining white as snow in the night around the circular clearing where the ornamental pavilion sat waiting, silent and mysterious under the moon.

Stephanie stopped at the edge of the clearing. She gazed at the pavilion.

"It's like a dream," she said.

Steve led her across the grass to the front door. He glanced up for a moment at Kwan-on — the Japanese goddess of mercy — then he tried the door.

It was locked.

"Does anyone live here?" asked Stephanie.

"Only in the daytime," he told her.

Steve walked along the front of the pavilion. "They've got some fantastic stuff in there. Great paintings."

He peered in at the bamboo-framed window, holding his hands, blinker-fashion, beside his eyes — but the slatted blinds were closed, and all he could see was his own reflection in the glass.

"They've locked it all up," he said.

There was a silence. She leaned her head against his shoulder. "Does it matter?"

"Not really."

"What were we going to do in there anyway?" she asked, mock-innocent. "Read T.S. Eliot?"

He kissed her fiercely then, and they stood wrapped in each other, swaying together. After a while she moved back and led him by the hand across the thick grass of the clearing. Moon shadows followed them across the clearing, and then vanished as she sat beneath a cherry tree, pulling him gently down with her. An owl flew out between two trees, surprising Steve. He watched it swoop low and then rise, wings beating fast and silently as the bird hunted in the night.

"I hate owls," said Steve.

Stephanie did not answer. She was gazing at him with an intensity which was almost religious. She raised her hand to his face.

"I want you so much," she whispered. "I want to be you."

He turned to her then, and laid T.S. Eliot's *Collected Poems* down on the grass. They could still hear the love song, clear and distant in the night.

A wave of thunderous applause broke out across the lawn as the song ended. The black superstar bowed and returned the microphone to the Jamaicans. She tried to step down from the verandah, but the guests would not allow it; they crowded forwards and pushed her laughing back onto the stage amid a chorus of praise and shouts for an encore. She raised her sinewy arms in feigned surrender and ducked out of sight for a conference with the musicians.

I could see that the party was livening up, and I was giving a lot of thought to the idea of standing up and joining it. I could see Howard by the pool, thoughtfully throwing ice cubes into the water while Kathy talked quietly and earnestly into his ear. Joey was waving his arms at Susie — who appeared to have taken all her clothes off. I supposed she was about to jump into the pool. I remembered reading somewhere that at music parties everything always ended up in the pool, so we had that to look forward to. I could just make out the white bulk of Milton Rubin, prostrate on a chaise longue. There was a girl kneeling before him; she looked like Kate. I thought really I must talk to Howard about those two girls because maybe there was still time to interchange them — though I knew that, if I did not move fairly soon, there would be no question of interchanging anyone that night. On that thought, I closed my eyes. Another round of applause heralded the black superstar's encore and, as she began to sing the title number from the *Self-Made Man* album, I fell asleep again.

Steve and Stephanie heard it too: faintly yet distinctly in the clearing before the Japanese pavilion. White clothes were strewn around the clearing now, on the grass which shone blue in the moonlight as they made love.

Steve was lying behind and above her. She was face downwards, arms outstretched on either side. Her fists were clenching and unclenching and her head was lifted up, as far back as she could raise it so that her chin was clear of the grass and there was a small vein in her neck which throbbed in rhythm with the clenching and unclenching of her fists. Her eyes were shut and her mouth was opening and closing in time with the forwards and downwards movement of her back.

Their bodies seemed fused together in a perfect unison of movement, and when Steve lowered his head to hers from the darkness above and their identical profiles slowly overlapped they seemed like reflections in a pool of water which the wind has disturbed — and when their profiles finally coincided one upon the other they matched exactly like the head on a coin and for that moment they seemed truly one being, superimposed one upon the other as on the cover of the *Reflections* album.

And they were so completely one and one movement that there seemed no reason why they should not go on indefinitely (or at least until the song ended) except that Stephanie's fists suddenly clenched and would not open, her outstretched arms became taut, her mouth opened and would not close and the hollowing of her back slowed, then stopped altogether, her shoulders began to shake and she gasped aloud once, twice, then lowered her head towards the grass and shouted. She shouted twice, but the second time she muffled it in the grass. After some time her fists unclenched and she laid her face sideways on the grass, and soon after that the vein in her neck stopped throbbing.

Steve lay on top of her for a while, without moving. He gazed down at her face — the closed eyes, the happy mouth with the blonde hair strewn across it. Eventually she opened her eyes, twisted her face up towards him, and kissed him.

"Did I scream?" she asked.

He moved her hair away from her mouth and smiled.

"I suddenly wanted you to strangle me," she added. "I've never felt anything like that before."

After a while she raised herself gently, forwards and sideways — sliding out from underneath him. Then she sat up, cross-legged, and stared at him intently.

[159]

"I always knew it wasn't true."

"You knew what wasn't true?"

He was leaning up on one elbow, his face in a shadow.

"All that stuff about you being gay and useless and all. I had an instinct about that."

"Useless?"

"People are jealous is all. If they can't have something, they must knock it. I guess you've always been choosy, right?"

He paused, looking at her. "Useless, you said?" The word seemed to have some special significance for him.

"It's like when people can't understand something they give it a name they can understand."

"But that particular word," he insisted. "Useless — who said that?"

He had stopped smiling now and he was sitting up out of the shadow and seeing the trees and hearing the music and frowning in a puzzled way as though trying to remember something.

"Nobody said that — I mean, I said it, but only because that was what — hey, you're not mad, are you? I only told you that because you know, you're really so fantas—"

"But someone did say that —" he interrupted. "Who was it?"

His puzzlement was changing rapidly to an unaccountable agitation. "And it was nighttime and my music was playing — when was that?"

He suddenly hit the grass hard and frustrated with his fist as he made a huge recollective effort:

In his mind a girl's voice was echoing, echoing, full of scorn "Useless, useless, jesus you are fucking useless" and there was the moon and pine trees and the distant sound of the *Self-Made Man* album and it was a memory that had been hovering on the edge of his mind all day and now it was there, he could see it and he could hear it but it would not focus would not would not still would not focus —

[160]

"Steve, listen —"

Stephanie put both her arms around him and pressed her forehead against his neck, saying, "That was the most beautiful sexual experience I ever had in my life. How could I be so dumb as to —?"

Steve interrupted her by moving onto his knees and reaching for his clothes. "I've been trying to remember something all day," he told her.

He stood up and pulled on his white trousers.

"And if I could only just — get it, I'd —"

He paused, hearing the distant wave of applause as the song ended. The stars shimmered. The pavilion looked like a stage setting beneath them. The applause died away and there was a silence.

And then something clicked in his mind.

"Christ," he said.

Everything was clear to him at last, in the silence.

"So that's who she was."

He turned to Stephanie and, as she testified later to Superintendent Kellerman, that was the first and only time she remembered seeing Steve afraid.

42

Images formed in Steve Rice's mind:

The yellow Ferrari looked ivory-colored in the moonlight as it swerved into the narrow lane off Coldwater Canyon Drive. The stereo played the title track from the *Self-Made Man* album as Carol braked to a halt, switched off the lights and the engine. The top was down, and she lowered the volume of the music before turning her full attention to Steve.

He was sitting back in the low seat, his head back as he stared up at the silvery trees. He smiled a contented smile, vague and dreamy. His face was pale in the moonlight, ash-blond hair bleached almost white — like a fallen angel. He looked at her from blue-violet eyes, the pupils hugely enlarged — and when she leaned across and kissed him inaccurately on the mouth he did not move at all. Carol sat back and loosened her Hermès scarf.

"Did you like that?"

"I've never seen the sky so near," he said. He was staring up, through the trees.

"That's not all that's near," she told him.

Carol opened her crocodile bag with the golden *C* on it and took out a pack of Virginia Slims. She tipped one out and offered it to Steve, but he did not see it. She put the cigarette between her lips, replaced the pack in her bag and took out her gold Dunhill lighter. She continued to look at Steve across the flame as she lit the cigarette, and afterwards the light in the car paled again and was flecked with blue smoke which drifted slowly upwards towards the pines.

"I wasn't outside that window by chance, you know?" she said. "I saw you were escaping! I watched you go into the john then I ran out and around the house and waited. Brilliant, huh?"

There was a wave of taped applause as the title track ended, followed by a moment's silence.

Steve did not move. Carol peered at him, then passed a hand in front of his face. "Hey, remember me? Your savior, Carol Berenson?" She picked up his limp hand and shook it.

"Have you read any Eliot?" he asked her.

"Eliot who?" (Then she thought he meant George Eliot, but it did not really make too much difference.)

"Do you remember what he said about stillness?"

"Stillness?"

" 'As a Chinese jar still moves perpetually in its stillness.' "

"Ah-ha."

She waited attentively for him to go on but apparently that was it. Steve was lost in his own world now — drifting serenely through space, through an artificially produced universe without pain or aggression, without violence or ego or desire. He had taken exactly the right amount for the day and felt himself verging on the peace and tranquillity of the saints.

Carol shifted in her seat. For her part, she had drunk a bottle of champagne that night and its effect on her had very little to do with either stillness or tranquillity. "I guess you and I reversed the normal roles, didn't we?"

He turned his eyes towards her.

"I felt like you were the damsel in distress, and I was the knight in the shining Ferrari!"

She giggled at this — the concept pleased her; then she laid her cigarette in the ashtray and leaned towards him.

"I wanted you the moment I saw you," she whispered. "As soon as you walked onto that stage. I practically came just watching you."

She began to undo the buttons on his black silk shirt.

[163]

"And I always get what I want, like Daddy taught me." She slipped one hand inside his shirt. "Not that he'd approve of this — but he won't know because we've been so brilliant."

"Yes, uh, listen —" Steve sat up straighter. "I thought we were driving along the beach?"

"The beach is too crowded," she told him. "Full of people screwing."

"So where are we?"

"Coldwater Canyon. On a hot night." She undid the rest of his shirt buttons. "My secret place since I was fourteen."

She slid both hands along his chest and sighed deeply.

"But haven't we both been brilliant? No one saw us together! Daddy will never know, and neither will Howard. He's real jealous, that little grafter. I'll never marry him either, you can bet on it — or anyone else if I can help it."

She kissed Steve rather sloppily on the mouth, and then, before he could protest:

"Just relax, Steve. Lean back on the seat. On my leather maroon seat! How do you like my little Ferrari? Isn't this the neatest birthday present you ever saw? Sure, Daddy spoils me, but why not? That's his philosophy. 'Have it now,' he says. 'We're not around for long.' So I have it. All of it. And now I have you. Brilliant. Daddy should be proud. My first hijack job." She giggled. "You've probably never had a hijack job, Steve."

"Let's get out of the car," he said.

"What for?"

"I need some space."

"Listen, the ground's hard out there, and there could be snakes."

"We can walk."

"Walk? Jesus."

As he reached for the door handle, she said: "One final detail, huh? One brilliant *numero-uno* detail you should know about. When I push this little lever, so — the whole thing just kind of —" She tipped the lever and the leather seat-back sank away to the horizontal. "Isn't that brilliant?"

Steve stayed sitting up but Carol climbed all over him, giggling and pushing him down until his claustrophobia built to such a point that at last he tipped her sideways against the steering wheel, shoved open the car door and stepped out onto the dried-up, stubbly grass of Coldwater Canyon.

He stood there swaying slightly, drawing deep breaths and staring up at the moon. Carol sat in the car, blinking at him. Finally she shrugged.

"OK," she said. "I know an old Indian cure for snakebite."

She stepped out of the Ferrari and crossed to him, arms folded high on her shoulders.

"Come and see the view."

She walked along the edge of the pine forest. After a few yards the thick, shadowy scrub sloped away and Steve found himself staring clear across the San Fernando Valley, to where the blue pinpoints of light seemed hardly bigger than the stars.

"There!"

Carol waved at the horizon with the air of someone who had conjured it up out of nowhere at very short notice; then, leaning heavily against him —

"I lost my virginity on this very spot," she told him.

Steve stood still, hearing the music from the car stereo and looking out to where the gray mountains rose beyond the valley, banking up like a great auditorium against the sky. I can only guess at his thoughts at that moment — but I do recall that once, after the concert in Denver, Steve told me of a vision he had one night while out of doors with a girl (he remembered the vision, not the girl) — and I like to imagine that it was now. He had been staring at some far-off hills and all at once the tiny lights began to seem like eyes to him — eyes that watched him — the countless thousand eyes of expectant fans glittering at him from the hostile darkness, and he felt abruptly afraid, wondering how he would ever be able to perform for such a cosmic audience —

The girl was on her knees before him and had both arms around his legs while he stared into the darkness. Then he heard the clapping — the thunder of applause swelling and roaring and echoing in the hills; the lines of lights blurred and refocused as Steve saw himself ghostlike in the sky, arms fallen from his guitar, eyes closed, face raised to the single spotlight of the moon. It was only when he bowed his head in acknowledgment of the applause that the first dark-red arrow shaft appeared from the center of his chest. It was there so suddenly that it seemed to have come from inside him. He took hold of the shaft with both hands and was trying to pull it out when two more shafts struck him, one in the hip and one in the neck. After that he revolved slowly and helplessly in the sky beneath a hail of arrows from the surrounding blackness. The vision ended as — impaled a dozen times, like Saint Sebastian in the Mantegna portrait — his blood-soaked image dissolved to nothing above the distant hills.

Then he was on the ground, lying on the tough, scratchy grass with the unknown girl on top of him. She had clicked off his turquoise buckle and opened the Tibetan belt while he was still recovering from this premonition of death in the California night. She forced down his zip, and the black pants with it, and he could feel her hands on him and his total absence of desire and he tried to pull away but she was lying across his knees and for the moment he could not move. Then he felt her mouth against his thigh — the soft warm lips moving up, the mobile tongue and the guiding hand, and he lay back and tried to relax because he had always enjoyed that in the past; but tonight it was not any good and whatever she did to him made no difference. He could not concentrate on what she was doing to him anyway, and he just lay there staring at the trees and wondering if what he had seen could possibly be some kind of psychic feedback from the mind of T.S. Eliot, whose early, visionary works had deeply influenced his teens: the masochistic poems about Saint Sebastian and Saint Narcissus — solitary men who sought and found the deaths they desired, in each case involving the violent annihilation of their physical beauty . . .

A harsh voice disturbed this reverie:

"Useless!" the voice exclaimed. "Jesus, you are fucking useless!"

He looked down to where the branches cast strange shadows on the dry grass. A girl knelt among them, but he had no idea of who she was.

"The hotshot superstar," she went on. "A great big nothing!" She laughed briefly. "And I mean nothing."

Steve sat up. "I feel weird."

"To me you feel like nothing," she told him. "A big useless nothing." She laughed again.

Steve stood up, fastening the turquoise belt-buckle.

"Let's go," he said.

"We'll go when I'm ready."

"Listen," he explained, "I don't like it here. I'm not 'appy. Let's go."

"Sit down." She grabbed one of his legs. "It's my car, I hijacked you, and you must be good for something."

Steve turned brusquely but she held his leg firmly, wrapping both arms around it. "Oh come on, for Christ's sake —"

He swung his booted leg, pulling her along the ground. She seemed to enjoy this, and started to giggle — until he freed himself with a sudden kick out and away from her. After that she lay on the grass while he marched back to the Ferrari. As he reached it, she climbed to her feet, leaned against a tree, and shouted:

"Just my luck, huh? Wouldn't you know it? I hijack the great god of fuck and what do I get? Nothing. A fucking

[167]

useless nothing. What are you, hotshot? Besides being useless?"

Steve stepped into the car and leaned his head back, hearing
her voice echo — "useless, useless" — through the canyon.
She was shouting more things as she walked towards him, her
face flushed and angry, and he turned up the volume of the
stereo to try to drown out the derisive voice but it came
through anyway:

"You're not a faggot by any chance? You're not by any
chance a useless British faggot? I mean you're so pale and
poetic and full of shit about Chinese vases —"

Steve doubled the volume of the *Self-Made Man* tape. He
was breathing rapidly now. His chemical serenity had been
dangerously disturbed — first by claustrophobia, then visual
fallacies, now this stream of abuse; he was sinking into a
paranoid confusion. He scarcely knew where he was or what
was happening: only that he must get away.

"So maybe I had it right about the damsel in distress? But
what a joke, huh? Every girl's dream a useless British fairy.
That is if you can even get it up with boys — can you, Steve?
Can you make it with anyone? Tell me the truth!"

Beside the stereo, a gold key jutted from the ignition. Steve
slid across to the driver's seat and sat down on Carol's crocodile bag. He pulled it from beneath him and hurled it in her
general direction.

She shouted "Hey!" and half caught the bag — then
dropped it, whereupon the contents spilled out all over the
grass. While she was gathering them up Steve twisted the key,
the engine started and he shoved the selector lever to reverse.
Carol looked up when the engine fired and she straightened
in time to watch her car swerving backwards onto Coldwater
Canyon Drive.

"What're you doing?" she yelled. "Come back here!"

She stumbled after the car as it bumped out onto the main

road, where Steve braked momentarily, spinning the steering wheel.

"OK —" she called, "you've made your point. I'm coming."

Even then it had not really occurred to Carol that he would leave without her, and she slowed to a walk as she approached the car. But after Steve moved the selector lever forwards without even glancing around, she found herself standing in the middle of the road, watching her own Ferrari disappear into the night. As it growled out of sight around the first sharp bend, she told herself this must be a joke, he was only doing it to scare her and get even and he would be back. But when the sound of the engine and the *Self-Made Man* tape had both died away to nothing and the deep silence of the canyon had settled down around her she began to wonder.

An owl quavered nearby — making her leap with fright. Carol started to sober up.

The Pacific Ocean shone smooth under the moon as Steve roared up the Coast Highway towards Malibu. He was aiming for Milton Rubin's house, but he pulled into the wrong driveway, dented the right front fender against the gatepost, swerved alongside the deserted frame house and skidded to a halt in the white sand of the private beach beyond. When he realized the mistake he shifted to reverse, but the tires spun in the sand, and there was nothing to do but switch off the engine and the stereo and wait for his head to clear. As soon as the car was silent he must have heard the sounds of the party drifting along the beach, but either he did not connect it with Milton Rubin's, or else the sea had already claimed him.

Steve had always been obsessed by the sight and sound and smell of the ocean. He told me once about his first view of it, at Brighton in England. He was thirteen at the time, and his parents had taken a cheap day-return fare from London.

As the train pulled into the station he could already smell the salt in the air and then, after he had run the length of a road and around a corner, there it was: vast, gray and troubled — the most romantic thing he had ever seen. He ran down onto the beach and among the rocks and the rock pools which the tide left as it went out. He spent all day there, hunting shrimps among the rocks and ducking the huge waves which broke and sprayed the people on the promenade. . . . He fell in love with the sea that day and his early songs were filled with images of sails and shipwrecks, rocks and storms —

So I expect that the sight of the Pacific, the greatest ocean in the world, stretching away before him that night, after all that had happened, must have seemed like some kind of a healing balm — and that by throwing off his black shirt and boots and pants and diving into that white surf he was in some way reliving the purification ceremonies of the ancients —

Afterwards I believe he slept as peacefully as a child on the warm sand — then rose with the sun and walked innocent and forgetful through the bright dawn to Milton Rubin's house, rejoining his friends in time to catch the morning flight back to London.

43

To Stephanie it felt as if Steve had just returned from a long journey.

The moon had risen higher, and its light lay white as a shroud across the Japanese pavilion as he stood in the clearing — understanding for the first time the danger that he was in. His fear communicated itself to her, and although she had still made no attempt to get dressed, she began to look around for her clothes —

Then she saw the three men.

At first they seemed like blue shadows, but they were moving forwards, and Stephanie saw them and she gasped. Steve followed her gaze, and called:

"Who's that?"

There was no answer from among the trees. The shadows advanced.

"Who are they?" whispered Stephanie.

"I don't know," he said.

They were spread out like hunters, with several yards between, and there was a tension between the men as they watched to see which way Steve would run. When they realized that he would not run at all they spread out farther until they had surrounded him and then they stepped out from the darkness of the trees into the white light of the clearing.

The first was thin-faced, his features shadowed by the peak of his military-style cap; the second was hook-nosed, dark and burly; the last was round-faced, his steel-framed spectacles glinting in the moonlight. All three wore rough workman's clothes, denim overalls, leather jackets. Stephanie stared at them.

"Who are they?" she cried. "What do they want?"

"We'll soon find out."

Steve seemed curiously calm at that moment, and unafraid, as they closed around him. The only sound was the measured swish of their footsteps.

Stephanie panicked then, snatching up her shirt and her white trousers and making a dash for the pathway. She stumbled, tripped and then recovered herself in time to fall straight into the arms of the spectacled man, who held her easily, one thick arm pinioning hers, his broad hand cutting off her scream. She struggled furiously, dropping her clothes and making deep choking noises in her throat. Steve objected to this:

"Hey!" he shouted. "Let 'er go, you fucking bully!"

He ran to help her, but the other two men caught him and spun him around, and then the thin-faced one gave him a shove in the chest which sent him staggering backwards towards the bamboo-framed window of the pavilion.

Stephanie put up as good a fight as could be expected of a girl who was stark naked and frightened to death — but the spectacled man soon gagged her with a small bath towel and then tied her hands and feet together with the cord he pulled out from the pocket of his overalls. He lifted her up, together with her clothes, and carried her across to the pavilion — setting her down beside the sliding door. He draped the clothes across her body and, when she had taken her last horrified look at Steve, he blindfolded her with a cotton scarf. After that he lost all interest in her, turning his attention towards the center of the clearing, where his colleagues were having an unexpected amount of trouble with Steve.

They discovered that, although slender, he was also wiry and quick. There was a residue of gutter toughness left over from the Brixton childhood, and — fuelled by his lifelong hatred of bully-boys — he was attacking so recklessly that at first he seemed to be driving them off. He kicked the thin-faced man in the stomach and landed an excellent punch to the hook-nosed-man's eye before they had fully recovered from their surprise — but after that they set about him with a frightening deliberation, as if they had the whole night before them. They took it in turns to hold him, while the other pounded fists into a fixed target. Three blows in the stomach brought Steve's head down. A knee to the face was timed to coincide with the downward crash of arms to the back of the neck. Then came the awful splitting sound as his nose broke and the grass around began to shine with blood. Steve toppled forwards onto the ground and lay there, doubled up and broken looking, hands to his face, clasping something intolerable. After that they kicked him for a while, concentrating on his ribs and spine, and then the hook-nosed man hauled him up and positioned him high in the air like a broken doll while the thin-faced man aimed a series of murderous punches to the groin.

Steve's head was lolling to one side, and his face was unrecognizable — but still they took it in turns to hold him while the other rained in the blows. There was a snapping sound as Steve's jawbone broke, and shortly after that they let him fall — but more because they needed a rest than for any other reason. They sat on the ground, breathing deeply and watching as Steve writhed and twisted, caught by something that seemed not to be there.

Then they all turned towards the Japanese pavilion —

Where Carol Berenson stood in the bamboo-framed window — a witness to it all.

The slatted blind had been raised and she stood in the window flanked by tall, shadowy figures on either side and a little behind her. Carol's ruined face seemed drained of blood in the terrible silence that followed the beating. It was the face of a woman in shock, a woman forced to reconfront the horrors of her own assault in Coldwater — to relive her own nightmare. She stood trembling and weeping and trying to cry out but a dark hand from behind had covered her mouth. She closed her eyes and tried to turn away, but after that J.P. moved forwards into the light and stood right beside her in the window, holding her gently, murmuring into her ear and insisting that she watch everything, everything —

The men returned to Steve, who was still scrambling and kicking on the ground. They did not beat him this time, but the thin-faced man pulled an oily rag from the pocket of his overalls and rammed it into Steve's blood-filled mouth. The spectacled man produced a silver scarf and tied his wrists together. After that they stripped the white trousers from his legs and hauled him up to a kneeling position —

It was when the hook-nosed man unzipped his own jeans and knelt down behind Steve that Berenson had to shift his hand to allow his daughter to throw up all over the pale green tatami floormat. He supported her while she vomited, stroking her hair and murmuring comfortingly as he had when she had been a child and had eaten too many cookies or cream-cakes at a party. He glanced across the dim interior of the pavilion to where Huey stood, staring out of the window, but Huey was too deeply absorbed by the rape to notice Carol's indisposition at all.

When the hook-nosed man was finished he rolled aside and lay panting on the grass, fastening his belt.

The other two lifted Steve to his feet, and it was while they were preparing to tie him to the cherry tree under which he had so recently made love to Stephanie that — calling upon unfathomable depths of outrage and courage — Steve produced a final lung-splitting burst of energy: crashing his head into the thin-faced man's chin and landing a swinging kick to the face of the recumbent rapist.

The thin-faced man staggered backwards, then recovered.

His military-style peaked cap fell to the ground, his long hair tumbled down and Steve — staring through the puffed-up remains of his eyes — found himself looking into the face of Huey's nephew Floyd.

The hook-nosed man knelt up, cursing and groaning. Steve's foot had caught him in the mouth — several capped teeth were gone and the false nose had been flattened. He peeled it away as he stood up, revealing — beneath the Shylock makeup — the bloodstained face of Jason.

When Steve felt himself gripped from behind he realized that of course this must be Jay with padded out cheeks and plain spectacles. He also realized that he had been set up for this encounter from the start. Not that he had long to think about it — for they came at him with renewed hatred now, and his eyes were soon completely closed, and his broken jaw hung slackly and wobbled obscenely each time it was struck.

Huey stood at the window, drawing on a cigar and watching his boys work over Steve Rice. Kwan-on, the Japanese goddess of mercy, smiled serenely from her alcove as they tied him to the cherry tree, attaching his wrists to a thick branch above his head.

When Floyd removed his wide, metal-edged belt, Huey turned to see how his employer's daughter was reacting to this — and found that she had fainted clean away. She lay on the floor of the pavilion, her head and shoulders cradled in J.P.'s lap. She was breathing evenly, her eyes were closed and her skin was the color of wax. Berenson was stroking her hair, straightening it and fluffing it out from her face.

The boys took it in turns to flog Steve with the metal-edged belt. Each blow was accompanied by a shower of snowy-white blossoms, as his head crashed forwards against the tree trunk. Huey exhaled smoke, stared up at the impersonal stars, then turned to J.P.

"I'd better stop them."

J.P. did not speak. Huey looked at him.

"Now Carol's passed out — it's either worked or it hasn't."

J.P. did not speak.

Huey peered more closely at J.P. across the dim Japanese interior. Then understood. He whistled to himself, and murmured, for the sake of routine, of good business procedure:

"They'll kill him if I don't."

Still stroking Carol's hair, Berenson turned to the window. As he looked out at the clearing, his eyes held that detached intensity which comes from the periodic contemplation of death.

He did not speak.

The only sound was the rhythmic thudding from the cherry tree.

Several hours later, when the first rays of the morning sun were coloring the ancient towers of the gatehouse at Avonhurst, a battered truck chugged into view along Benedict Canyon Drive. The truck slowed as it passed the gatehouse, the tarpaulin at the back was raised, and a large canvas duffel bag was thrown out. It hit the road heavily and rolled a few feet before settling to rest. The title page of T.S. Eliot's *Collected Poems* had been ripped out and pinned to the duffel bag. Across it had been printed the legend FORGIVE US OUR TRESPASSES.

BOOK THREE

44

Many months later, I recall the next morning simply as the worst one of my life.

It began badly enough, with a dream I was having about a black child who had been murdered, wearing my clothes. The police sirens seemed to be part of the dream — until the suspicion dawned within the dream that they were not. Next came the awful lurch back to reality as I opened my eyes and found myself staring up into the branches of a tree. I lay still for a while, inhaling the scent of crushed pine-needles, and wondering what on earth I was doing, out of doors, on the grass, under a pine tree. I could still hear the sirens. They sounded farther away than in my dream, but there were more of them and the noise was building.

I raised myself up a little and surveyed the lawn. The swimming pool reflected the poolhouse in the morning light. A colored lantern bobbed jauntily across the water, and there were many glasses and bottles shining in the sun. I remembered the party, and closed my eyes. I opened them and looked at my wristwatch. It was six-thirty. I sank heavily back onto the grass.

Several doors were thrown open on the south terrace, and all the telephones in the castle seemed to be ringing. I moved my head and watched a line of ants crawling up and down the tree trunk beside me. Voices were raised and there was the sound of people running. I heaved myself up again, and saw the majordomo hurrying down the steps and off in the direction of the unicorn clearing. He was accompanied by three servants and they were all carrying shotguns.

Someone had switched on a radio, and a news bulletin crackled along with the telephones in the castle. As fast as one telephone was answered another one rang, but I was too far away to hear what was said — especially above the unnaturally loud bird-song of that morning. I stayed propped up for a while, watching dark shadows swoop across the lawn as birds hunted insects in the dawn.

There was the sound of tires in the courtyard and a slamming of car doors, and four T-shirted security men raced each other through the bougainvillea-covered archway, across the lawn and off in the direction taken by the majordomo. A line of servants had gathered on the terrace, and they were all smoothing their hair and buttoning their clothes as though they had been unexpectedly awakened. Ace, the chauffeur, was talking to the headwaiter, who kept waving his one and only arm in the direction of the Japanese pavilion.

When the gardener came running from the direction of the unicorn clearing, I sat up properly, holding on to my knees. The man was panting and stumbling and shouting in Spanish. I made out the word *robado*, which I guessed meant "stolen" — so perhaps there had been a robbery during the night. He kept on shouting whatever it was over and over again, and was still shouting as the headwaiter led him up the terrace steps and into the castle.

The telephone beside the pool began to ring and, while I was staring at that, all the telephones in the poolhouse began to ring too. There was a much louder whooping of sirens from what I now realized was the direction of the gatehouse. I rubbed my face vigorously, trying to get my eyes open. I looked up at the light which filtered softly through the pine branches. The paper lantern had been ripped apart and the electric bulb was covered with scorched insects — their death wish had been granted.

I thought: I must go to our room and see Kathy. But then two more gardeners appeared from the direction of the unicorn clearing carrying what looked to be a body, wrapped in a Japanese kimono. Ace the chauffeur led them towards a chaise longue by the pool, where they set the bundle down.

Placing one hand on the grass, I pushed myself up and walked across to the pool. Several servants had come down from the terrace and were standing around the chaise longue. I looked down at the perfect, unmarked face and thought for a moment that it was Steve; but then the face moved and mumbled something and I could see that it was Stephanie.

The poolhouse door burst open and Howard appeared, wearing only a white bath-towel. He was angry at having been woken up.

"What the fuck's going on?" he demanded.

Ace told him gently: "There's been another killing."

Howard stared at him, then at the kimonoed figure. "Stephanie?" He bent over the chaise longue and lifted her head. She moaned, turning her face from side to side. "What happened?"

"She's been tied up all night," said Ace. "The pavilion's been busted open and a whole bunch of jade's been stolen."

Howard looked at him, trying to comprehend this.

"Plus someone's dead in a duffel bag out on Benedict," Ace shrugged. "Kellerman's coming over."

Carol's nurse pushed through the ring of servants, set her first-aid box down on the chaise, felt Stephanie's forehead and then her pulse. Joey came out of the poolhouse, buttoning up his shirt. His hair was uncombed, and he looked terrible. He saw Stephanie, and stood quite still. We all watched while the nurse passed some ammonium carbonate under her nose, and after a moment she began to revive. Her huge eyes opened: they were pale blue in the daylight. She looked around and tried to sit up but the nurse restrained her. The kimono fell apart and the nurse closed it, tying the sash and adjusting a pillow behind her back.

"Just lie still, honey," said the nurse. "Until the doctor comes."

Stephanie sank back onto the cushion, putting her hands over her eyes. That was when we saw the dark red marks on her wrists. Howard knelt beside her.

"Listen baby," he whispered urgently. "What happened?"

She sobbed, and shook her head.

"Can you talk?" He looked at the nurse. "Can't she talk?"

"She should be quiet, Mister Vance. Until the doctor comes."

"Stephanie baby," insisted Howard. "What happened, huh? Where's Steve?"

At the mention of Steve's name she wailed and rolled over with her back to us all.

"So quit now," suggested the nurse, "until the doctor comes."

Stephanie lay still, with her knees drawn up and her hands pressed against her face. Howard rose to his feet. He looked at me; his eyes held the same dread that I had felt all the day before.

"Let's check his room," suggested Joey.

Howard nodded, and they crossed the lawn together.

I walked up the verandah steps and through the sliding glass doors into the poolhouse. It was cool and dark in there, and most of the blinds were closed. I crossed towards the bathroom, passing a large divan bed on which I saw Susie and Kate, peacefully asleep, entwined in each other's arms. So Howard and Joey had interchanged them after all. I wondered who had watched whom.

I went into the bathroom and opened the blinds. There was a pair of white panties on the floor. I picked them up and placed them on the bidet. I turned to the basin and stared at myself in the mirror. It was not a pleasant sight. I turned on the cold tap and splashed water on my face for a long time. I was trying to feel better, to feel less nauseous, and above all not to think —

I was already quite sure of where they would find Steve Rice.

45

J.P. Berenson woke up in his silk bedroom
to the soft buzzing of the housephone. He lifted the receiver,
taking care not to disturb the woman asleep beside him. He
listened for a moment, then said,

"I'll come down."

He turned in the massive bed of black carved wood, once
owned by a Long Island bootlegger and, before that, by Car-
dinal Richelieu. Daylight filtered dimly through heavy curtains, embroidered with a medieval hunting scene. Before
getting out of bed, he lay propped up on one elbow, staring
at the woman beside him. It was Kathy. She slept as quietly
as always — mouth slightly open, auburn hair strewn over the
pillow — with just an occasional sigh when she changed position. He stroked her hair, straightened it and fluffed it out
from her face. She stirred a little, and murmured in her sleep.

J.P. rose from the bed and walked off to his dressing room.

A black-and-white squad car braked in the courtyard and
parked beside an ambulance. Two backup units pulled in
behind it, followed by a fourth car containing photographers,
fingerprint men, and a forensic chemist from the Scientific
Investigation Division of the Los Angeles Police Department.
Superintendent Kellerman descended from the first car and
walked towards the bougainvillea-covered archway. After him
came a lieutenant, a sergeant, the SID men, and six police
officers (two of whom were leading Alsatian dogs on chain
leashes).

I came out of the poolhouse in time to see the majordomo greet them all at the archway.

Kellerman and the lieutenant hurried over to the swimming pool, while the others followed the majordomo off towards the Japanese pavilion.

Stephanie had been given an injection. A police doctor in a white jacket was taping an adhesive plaster to her upper arm. The nurse was rubbing cream into her wrists. The glasses and bottles had been cleared from the swimming-pool area, and the lieutenant moved everyone back from the chaise longue, making space for the superintendent.

"Who found her?" asked Kellerman.

The gardener who had been shouting in Spanish raised his hand.

"What's your name?"

"Anselmo."

"How did you find her, Anselmo?"

"I go for work at lake and I pass *iglesia*," he began.

"He means the Japanese pavilion," said the headwaiter.

"I see door open. Smash open. In salon I find much disorder. I hear much noise, like, uh —" Anselmo kicked the side of the chaise to illustrate the noise.

"Where did the noise come from?"

"From cupboard."

"She was kicking at the door," said the headwaiter.

"I find her inside cupboard and she is, uh — uh —" He opened his mouth and pointed into it.

"Gagged," said the headwaiter.

"And blinded."

"Blindfolded," said the headwaiter.

"Also roped," said Anselmo, holding his wrists firmly together.

"These two carried her over." The headwaiter indicated the other gardeners. "Then we called you."

"What's been stolen?" asked the lieutenant.

[185]

"A shelf full of jade. Worth maybe half a million."

Kellerman nodded, and turned his attention to Stephanie. He looked down at her ash-pale face.

"Can you talk?"

Stephanie focused on him; the tranquillizing injection was beginning to work.

"Is she hurt?"

"She's jittery," replied the doctor.

"They didn't hurt me," said Stephanie.

Howard and Joey rejoined the group. Howard was wearing a warm-up suit now; he must have stopped off at his own room.

"Can you tell us who they were, Stephanie?" asked Kellerman, gently.

"I don't know. There were three of them. Steve didn't know, either."

"Steve?" Kellerman sounded startled.

"He's not in his room, Kellerman." Howard's voice was hoarse. He was sweating, and looked like a man whose entire world is collapsing around him.

Stephanie began to sob again.

"I think they killed him," she said.

Kellerman and the lieutenant looked at each other. Whatever theories they may have evolved by that point, they had clearly not anticipated this.

J.P. Berenson crossed the lawn, and everyone moved, making a path for him.

"I hear I've been robbed," he said.

"There's a homicide too, sir," said Kellerman. "The same type of duffel bag, with a note attached, dumped outside your gatehouse at six-fifteen. Your own security men called us. They saw the truck but not the plates."

Berenson was looking at Stephanie. The doctor had persuaded her to drink something from a plastic flask, and she had stopped sobbing.

"Where is the duffel bag?" asked J.P.

"On its way to the Coroner's Office," replied Kellerman. Then he added, aside — "Whoever's in there's really carved up."

I turned away and looked up at the sky, which was high and clear with the promise of another fine day. A hawk side-slipped into the breeze and then rose again. I watched the bird hunting above the line of the distant pine forest.

Kellerman perched on the end of Stephanie's chaise longue. J.P. picked up a wicker stool and sat beside her. I stood with Howard, Joey, Ace, the lieutenant and the nurse; we formed a semicircle around her. With the arrival of J.P, the headwaiter had moved the gardeners and servants back onto the verandah of the poolhouse, where they watched and waited in deferential silence.

"What did they look like, Stephanie?" asked Kellerman.

"Well, uh — one of them had spectacles, and kind of a round face. He tied me up. And another one — he wore a peaked cap."

Stephanie shivered, and was suddenly lost in thought. It was as though she had forgotten us. Kellerman prompted her: "And the third?"

"Huh?"

"What was the third one like?"

"He was darker. Kind of foreign-looking."

"I thought you were blindfolded, Stephanie?" said the lieutenant.

"Not until after I was tied up," she told him.

"So you had time to see them?"

"Too much time."

Kellerman asked her: "What makes you think they killed Steve?"

"It just sounded that way. He made a big fight at first, but then they got him and it just sounded like — oh, God —"

"Like what?"

"Like they were beating him to death."

"Have you heard many people beaten to death?" asked the lieutenant.

"Take it easy, Bob," Kellerman told him. Then, to Stephanie — "Just tell us what you heard."

"I heard them beating him. There was a kind of a cracking noise. Then I thought they must be whipping him, or hitting him with a log or something."

"Did anyone speak?"

"Not a word. That was another creepy thing."

"What else?"

"There was kind of a crash, right beside me."

"Could that have been the door going?"

"Maybe."

"Then what?"

"Then nothing."

In the silence which followed I stared at Berenson — at his pallor and his glittering eyes and I knew that he had willed it. I knew it absolutely. How and why, I could not guess. Could he conceivably have captured three homicidal truckers — who had eluded the police for a year — and coerced them into an act of almost Shakespearian revenge? It seemed impossible, but looking at him, I felt again the numbing sensation that for this man nothing would be.

He felt my eyes upon him, and he turned: and he saw that I knew. He returned my gaze quite coolly, even nodding slightly — as if to acknowledge my thoughts. Then he returned to Stephanie.

"It could be," Kellerman was saying, "that they came to rob the place and you just happened to be in the way."

"Strange night for a robbery," said Howard. "With two hundred guests here."

"Not really." Kellerman shrugged. "Plenty of noise, plus you had all the security on the gate."

"And how did they get in? There's a six-foot-high electric fence around the whole place."

There was a brief silence. No one had an answer for that.

"Let's finish with Stephanie," suggested the lieutenant, turning to her. "As I understand it you're employed by Mister Vance here for publicity reasons because you look like Steve Rice. And when you met Steve for the first time at ten o'clock last night, you gazed into his eyes and bells began to ring. Correct?"

She nodded, and I thought: poor kid. With her hair all dank and straight and no makeup she did not look nearly so much like Steve as at that enchanted moment the night before.

"Was that part of the deal?"

"What?"

"The ringing bells?"

"No. It wasn't." Stephanie looked as if she were about to cry again.

"It really wasn't," said Howard.

"All right, Bob," Kellerman interrupted. "That's not the point. The point is they ended up at that pavilion." He looked directly at Stephanie. "Why?"

"Why what?"

"Why the Japanese pavilion?"

"I asked to see it."

"You asked?"

"I'd heard about it. That it was very famous."

"Who told you that?"

"One of the reggae boys."

I thought: brilliant. So much for Steve and Stephanie just "happening" to be by the pavilion. I wondered how much richer that reggae boy was today.

"But Steve was going there anyhow," she added.

"He'd heard about it too?" asked the lieutenant.

"Steve knew the pavilion," said J.P. quietly.

There was another silence.

"Did you try to get in?" asked Kellerman.

"Yes, but it was locked."

"Were you planning to make it in there?"

"I guess so."

"What happened then?"

"We sat on the grass."

"And made it there instead?"

"Yes."

"Then the guys arrived?"

"Not right away."

"How much later?"

"God, who knows —"

"Five minutes? An hour?"

"An hour, maybe."

"Anyhow, before you got dressed?"

"Yes."

"So then they gagged you, tied you up, blindfolded you — and did nothing else to you at all."

Kellerman shook his head. He was surprised by this, and so was I (although not for much longer). Apart from the question of how they got in and out of Avonhurst, it was the only loose end in a robbery-homicide which fitted together with the precision of a Chinese puzzle.

And what irony, I thought: Steve Rice falls in love with his own image in the night, and wanders oblivious down a predestined pathway to his own death. Next morning the image which has bewitched him sits bedraggled and tranquillized upon a chaise longue, transformed overnight into a perfect witness for the police —

"Who else is staying here?" asked the lieutenant.

"Well, there's Huey Stander and his nephew Floyd, and two friends of Floyd's —" J.P. glanced towards the castle. "They'll be down in a minute. Then there's Dave's wife Kathy, and my daughter Carol. That's it."

"How is Carol?" Kellerman's voice became solicitous.

"She had a disturbed night and she's been sedated. Carol should wake up, uh —" J.P. glanced at his watch, "in about an hour." He turned to the nurse. "I think you should go back to her now."

"Yes, sir."

The nurse walked away across the lawn, passing Huey, who came hurrying down the steps of the south terrace. He wore a blue towelling robe and looked worried. He was followed by Floyd, Jason, and Jay, all of whom wore swimming trunks, with towels slung around their necks.

"Hi John, what a terrible thing!" exclaimed Huey. "Can we help?"

"Not really."

"Is there much missing?"

"I haven't checked yet."

"Well listen, we don't have to leave tomorrow. I'll change the bookings."

"There's no need for that, Huey."

"But I mean, how did they get in? Why didn't we hear anything?"

Huey was pitching his voice too high, I thought. He sounded too concerned. I wondered if anyone else noticed that.

"Hey, look —" Floyd stepped towards the chaise longue. "Who's that?"

"Is that Stephanie?" asked Huey.

"What happened to her? Hey, Stephanie?"

Jay moved right up beside Kellerman, and squatted on his heels in front of Stephanie.

"What happened, huh?" he asked, his athlete's face full of pudgy sympathy.

"She's been tied up all night," Ace told him.

"Tied up?"

"Jesus."

"That's a hell of a thing."

"Are you feeling OK now? Can we help?"

"I just feel tired," said Stephanie.

"Did you get to see them?" asked Floyd. "The guys who tied you up?"

"I saw them."

"You did?"

"No kidding!"

This seemed to excite Floyd and Jay. But, I thought: Why are they overacting?

The doctor rose and began to pack his medical equipment. "I think she should sleep now."

The lieutenant looked at Huey. "You're leaving tomorrow?"

"Well," shrugged Huey, "if we can't help. I have to get back to New York. And the boys only came to meet Steve Rice."

"Which was great for us," said Floyd.

"A great experience," said Jay.

There was a small silence.

"You got along well, huh?" asked the lieutenant.

"We had some great talks," replied Floyd. "About music and painting and art and all."

"He was real friendly to us," said Jay.

"He wouldn't play tennis though."

"We'll ask him again before we leave."

"But we had some fine conversations."

"It was fine when he signed the girls' bras too. Wish I'd had my camera for that!"

I thought: They are talking too much. Why are they talking so much? And why are they lying?

The lieutenant considered the silent Jason. "Have you hurt your face?"

"Oh shit, man —" Jason spoke with difficulty. "It hurts like hell."

[192]

"He ran into a chair," said Jay.

"Another chair?" snorted Huey.

"Someone threw a chair in the swimming pool last night," explained Floyd, "and poor old Jason dived right on top of it."

Jason attempted a rueful grin, and I could see the gaps where his front teeth had been.

"We could sue that drunk!" exclaimed Jay.

"I doubt it," snapped Huey. He sounded annoyed. Then, to Jason — "You're lucky to be alive. You've been horsing around in that pool ever since we got here."

Jason nodded, and looked rueful again.

"I think the best thing might be to carry her in on the chaise," said the doctor.

"Right doc," said Floyd.

"Come on men," said Huey. "Let's do something useful for a change."

So Huey took the top of the chaise, Floyd took the foot, Jason and Jay steadied it on either side, and the four of them bore Stephanie carefully away across the lawn. The doctor followed.

Kellerman looked after them for a moment, then turned to the lieutenant. "I want you to go downtown, Bob. Take Mister Vance with you."

"Downtown?" Howard's voice rose.

He stared at the superintendent, then understood. "Oh, no!" He shook his head.

"I'm sorry Howard."

"I can't do it."

"You've known Steve Rice longer than anyone here."

"He has to be identified," said the lieutenant reasonably.

"Take Joey as well," added Kellerman.

"Why me?"

"For a second opinion."

I stayed silent, praying that no one would suggest a third opinion.

"Do I have to do that?"

"I'm sorry Howard."

"Wasn't there anything else in that duffel bag?"

"There was some white clothing, plus a book of poems. The title page of the book was ripped out and pinned to the outside of the bag with a message."

"Were the poems by Eliot?"

"Yes."

"Isn't that enough?"

"No."

Berenson asked, "What was the message?"

" 'Forgive us our trespasses.' "

Howard turned aside. He looked as if he were about to throw up. Even the lieutenant sounded sympathetic:

"Let's go, Mister Vance. Let's get it over with. It only takes a minute."

Howard regarded him, then nodded. "Come on, Joey."

Joey took a deep breath, and the three of them walked off towards the bougainvillea-covered archway.

"It's a hell of a thing to ask someone," remarked Kellerman.

J.P. turned to me. His eyes had become as blank as a cat's. "We have things to discuss, Dave."

"We do?"

"Could you come to my study after breakfast?"

"Why not."

But I felt no enthusiasm for the meeting. It sounded about as appealing as an invitation from my old headmaster to discuss my future — if any.

At that moment the poolhouse door flew open and Susie tottered out, blinking and shading her eyes against the morning light. She was wearing a man's shirt, and was still half asleep.

"Howard?" she called. "Where is everyone? What's going on?"

Kate emerged behind her, wearing nothing but a pair of sunglasses.

"Why's everyone up so early?" Kate began. Then she saw her father.

"My God, it's Daddy!"

She vanished back into the poolhouse.

"Daddy?" Susie focused startled eyes on her father. "What are you doing here?"

"I thought you girls were home in bed," said Kellerman, heavily.

"Oh, well —" Susie became suddenly nonchalant. "It got kind of late, so we stayed over."

"I'd like you to get dressed now, Susie."

"Why's everyone up so early?"

"There's been a robbery here." Kellerman spoke carefully. "I'd like you to get dressed now."

"A robbery?"

"And call your mother — will you do that for me?"

"Who got robbed?"

"I'll talk to you later. Will you tell your mother that you and Katie are still at Avonhurst, that you've seen me and that you're all right. Will you do that for me?"

"Sure, Daddy."

"Go and get dressed now."

"Breakfast is at eight o'clock," J.P. told her. "In the dining room."

"Oh," replied Susie. "Thank you."

She went back into the poolhouse, closing the door behind her. Kellerman brooded:

"Daughters," he said.

J.P. chuckled. "Come on, Ace."

Ace grinned, hitched up the bulky revolver he always wore

under his left arm, and the three of them walked off in the direction of the Japanese pavilion. Apart from the superintendent, we had all been considerably cheered by the incident.

At the same moment a trail of blood from the Japanese pavilion was leading a police tracking dog straight to a gaping hole in the electric fence which surrounded the estate. The fence had been professionally short-circuited, and heavy-duty wire cutters had been employed to cut a space wide enough for a man to crawl through. Beyond the fence, a narrow, rarely used lane wound around the southwesterly boundary of Avonhurst, connecting up with Benedict Canyon Drive some two miles south of the gatehouse. Fresh tire tracks on the dusty road were consistent with the type of truck described by Berenson's security men — so the official verdict was inevitable: the killers had forced the fence, tied up Stephanie, robbed the pavilion and murdered Steve. As a grisly afterthought they had trailed his body back through the fence and placed it in a duffel bag — which had been dumped outside the Avonhurst gatehouse at dawn, less than an hour after the last guest had departed.

The pavilion itself had been carefully ransacked. The sliding door had been forced, and twelve pieces of jade removed. The most valuable piece was an intricately carved Fei Tsui bracelet — alone worth more than the headwaiter's estimate of half a million dollars. Two officers from the Latent Prints Section, Scientific Investigation Division, LAPD, dusted the entire pavilion for prints, but since the only readable impressions turned out to belong to either Carol or her nurse, it was concluded that the burglars wore gloves.

A hundred yards south of the pavilion, a policeman came upon the beheaded corpse of a German shepherd dog. Half an hour later they found a second Avonhurst guard dog, its back broken across a fallen tree trunk. The intruders had taken no chances. And, as one of the officers remarked, "They sure weren't dog-lovers."

46

I walked slowly up the Palladian staircase
and turned left towards our room. I was about to go in when
I heard the sound of voices from along the corridor. I continued past the tapestries and paintings until I reached the
end of the corridor.

Around the corner, at the foot of the second staircase, I
saw Floyd, Jason and Jay. They were standing at the foot of
the wide staircase and they had the chaise longue propped
up between them. They were returning to the lawn, and they
had paused there after maneuvering down the staircase. They
were standing together, whispering and giggling together. I
could see for the first time how deeply bruised Jason's face
was, swollen up with the eye half closed — and at that moment
they reminded me of schoolboys sharing a secret; or, even
more, of actors finally off-camera, relaxing after their scene.

And I suppose it was through seeing them like that —
grouped together, so involved with each other, and full of
complicity — that the truth finally hit me: or anyway, the
outrageous intuition of the truth.

At first I dismissed it, turned around and walked back to
our room. But once born, the idea would not go away. It
explained so many things. I walked right past our room and
found myself again at the Palladian staircase. I stood there
thinking furiously, and the more I thought the clearer it all
became: that was why Huey had sounded false and the boys
had overacted and lied about Steve's attitude towards them.
Why Stephanie had not been assaulted and why she had only

been allowed to watch for a moment before being blindfolded. And, if Steve had truly put up a fight, that was why Jason's face was in such a mess —

Overcome by the vision of this murderous charade, I sat down on the top step of the staircase and exclaimed aloud. Then came a cheerful voice:

"Hi Dave — what's up?"

It was Floyd, backing towards me along the corridor, ahead of Jason and Jay. They were carrying the chaise. I groaned. "I feel terrible."

They all laughed. It was credible enough. I must have looked terrible.

"The cure for that is tennis," said Jay.

I rose and stepped aside as they tilted the chaise into position at the top of the stairs.

"So we'll call for you after breakfast."

"Don't bank on it," I replied.

"Howard tells me you have a tremendous backhand," said Floyd.

As I stood watching them negotiate the staircase, the last of my doubts disappeared down the stairs with them. I remembered it all then: J.P. and Huey standing on the dark steps of the castle while I rummaged for Steve's book in the back of the VW bus. The boys joining them, noticing me, and then vanishing into the castle. I had not seen any one of them again that night. Kellerman displaying the simplified sketches of the real truck-drivers — basis for the disguises. I wondered if the boys carried makeup in their Adidas tennis bags? And what of the homosexual murder at Hillcrest Drive? Was that all part of it too? I supposed so — a kind of pitiless curtain-raiser for the main event. Then there was Berenson's mock-resignation — so well judged to disarm suspicion: "It doesn't matter now." "It's all over." "I must get back to my own life —" and so on.

"But he's the son of his father!" The voice of the party guest boomed in my head. "He inherited a mob, so what do you want?"

I stood outside our door considering the final twist: that never in a hundred years would Kellerman or anyone else suspect the truth — because the true motive (as opposed to the false motive of the break-in) was too well obscured. Without the knowledge that Steve had been with Carol on the night she was attacked, no one would ever look for a connection between two such disparate characters as Steve Rice and J.P. Berenson — without that knowledge a man might search a lifetime and never see beyond the false clues of the cut fence, the missing jade, the dead dogs.

I opened our door. But why should he do it? I could only think of revenge — some kind of godlike retribution . . . But could that be all? Even if one accepted Steve's total responsibility for Carol's condition — still, to fake a break-in and a robbery, to stage an elaborate masquerade and a copycat murder, merely to square that account — it seemed excessive even by California standards. Surely there would have been simpler ways —?

I entered our bedroom, and all these thoughts flew from my mind. The blinds were open, the four-poster bed was empty. Kathy was not there and she had not slept there. I collapsed into an armchair and stared at the embroidered coverlet of that made-up bed. She had not been with Howard, which left only one possibility. No wonder J.P. considered that we had things to talk about.

At the same time, Carol Berenson opened her eyes beneath the yellow-and-black banners of her high-school bedroom. She lay quietly for a while, gazing at the banners, and at the graduation photos lining the wall. Then she sat up and glanced towards the adjoining kitchen, where the nurse was

[199]

preparing breakfast. Carol stepped out of bed, smoothed down her nightgown, and crossed to the window. She pushed it open and gazed out.

The air shimmered. A faint wind moved the pine needles. Above the pine trees two LAPD helicopters hovered and swooped, casting long shadows across the lawn and across the strung-out line of police and dogs — still working their way diagonally across the estate.

The nurse emerged from the kitchen, carrying a breakfast tray.

"Good morning!" She set the tray down on the bed. "It's going to be real hot again."

Carol did not turn; she continued to stare at the line of policemen.

The nurse looked at her, curiously.

Carol did not speak.

47

"It was all for her. I want you to know that."

J.P. Berenson stood at the mullioned window of his study. Beside him hung a tapestry of Agamemnon and Iphigenia. Two Monets glowed from the opposite wall.

"Well," I said. "Great."

I sat on a leather sofa, elbows on knees, staring at the pattern in the carpet. I had skipped breakfast and waited for J.P. in his study — having first anesthetized my physical ache with two ten-milligram Valium. At that point I really did not care whether I lived through the rest of the morning or not. Nothing J.P. said would change anything, I knew that; and I was resolved not to mention Kathy until he did. I would simply listen. I had nothing else to do.

"And no one meant to kill him, I want you to know that too." He turned from the window. "You're an honest man, Dave, and you deserve the truth."

I thought: Oh God not again.

"It was an accident. And quite unnecessary. Carol had already passed out."

"Carol?" I looked up.

"It was all for her."

I regarded him. His hawk eyes were clear and calm.

"Are you telling me Carol was there?"

"It was staged for her. It was the second part of a shock cure, as prescribed by a certain eminent neurologist who prefers to remain anonymous. And we truly hoped it would not be needed. I did not lie to you last night. We hoped it would be enough — to just confront her with Steve."

I still could not grasp it. "You're saying you made Carol watch while you — while Steve —?"

"While he was beaten as she was beaten. While he suffered as she suffered. That is the principle of the shock cure — to recreate as nearly as possible the traumatic event. The greater the accuracy, the greater the chance of a cure. So ours was based on an attack made last year — against a girl from Salinas — by the same men who assaulted Carol. The boys put on their drama-school makeup and impersonated those men — but unfortunately they went too far. Steve made a fight of it, and apparently they didn't like him much. He'd been very rude to them at lunch."

"Rude to them at lunch?" I repeated, incredulous.

Berenson shrugged. "In the end they tied him to a tree, as Carol must have been tied to a tree. And then — accidentally — he hit his head against the tree trunk."

There was a pause. I could hear bees buzzing outside the window, and the faint whine of a vacuum cleaner from the floor above.

"After that some friends of Huey's cut the fence and carried him out to the truck. The boys cleaned up and went back to the party. I'm told you were asleep by then."

I considered him, genuinely awed. He made it all sound so simple. But what sort of man was this, who combined ferocity with such a vast disdain for human values? Who assumed divine rights, and then implemented them with such ruthless ingenuity? More than a law unto himself, J.P. Berenson had behaved like his own god. Or perhaps like his own father.

"And has it worked?" I asked.

He breathed in and out once. "We don't know yet." He glanced at his watch. "We have taken a great risk."

I rose from the sofa and wandered aimlessly across the room. I stared at a photograph of Carol, smiling from the ski slopes. The caption read *Aspen, Colorado '75.*

"What's to stop me talking to Kellerman?"

"Nothing," Berenson shrugged. "But he won't believe you."

"I might convince him."

"He'll think you're an overimaginative British playwright, deranged by grief."

"I can be very convincing."

"I'm sure of it, Dave. But Kellerman has everything he needs. He even has an eyewitness."

Yes, I thought, Stephanie was the masterstroke. Not only had she provided the bait, but she had also provided a false testimony of total conviction, coming as it did from a girl innocent of all deception herself. And again I marvelled at the sheer skill with which the trap had been sprung — the psychological insights, the accuracy with which reactions had been predicted: Had anyone so much as doubted that Steve's mirror image would hold the power to lead him anywhere? (And if not, well, no doubt there were alternative locations for the shock cure —)

"And, even if you did convince him, he'd never admit it. Or act on the conviction. Believe me."

Berenson sat down on a leather chair beside the door. He looked suddenly tired.

"So, Dave. I've paid you the compliment of telling you everything."

"Because I'm an honest man and deserve the truth?"

"Not entirely. There is also the question of your wife."

"Ah," I said. "Where is she?"

"Still asleep." He hesitated. "I want you to know we discussed you for hours last night."

I turned away.

"Neither of us has gotten into this thing lightly."

"Just quickly."

"It happened quickly. From the moment she stood by the pool — admiring the castle —"

"Well," I said, "she comes from Wiltshire too." I was not sure that I could bear much of this; certainly not the romantic details.

"Don't look like that." He stood up. "Can I get you something? You've had no breakfast —"

"I'm all right."

"We could have deceived you. We thought it best to be honest."

"Of course."

"I feel badly about it, God knows. And so does Kathy." He began to move around the room. "But I'd feel a whole lot worse if I didn't know your marriage was on the rocks anyhow. It's hard to say these things, but look — after Howard there would have been others. Kathy needs someone to take care of her, and you're at a point in your life when you need to be free."

"Free?"

"To climb out of the rut you're in. You're thirty-five years old and your career is in poor shape. An unhappy wife is no advantage to you now. You must be your own man, fulfill your own potential. Between the appreciated writer and the unappreciated one, the line is very fine. I want to help you cross that line."

Here it comes, I thought: the payoff.

"Yesterday afternoon, while you were playing tennis, Kathy showed me your logbook of the tour. I was most impressed by the work, by the thoroughness, the feeling for detail. Nothing escapes you, Dave. Nothing is too small for you to evaluate and consider. Now these are great qualities, and they are the qualities of a biographer: which happens to be what I need at the moment."

He moved behind his desk, abruptly businesslike. "I've decided that my family has been mysterious long enough. My father's passion was for secrecy, but he was a great man. He did things for America which no one has ever realized. It's time they did."

J.P. handed me a framed photograph. It showed a gaunt, somber-looking man standing on the White House lawn beside Franklin D. Roosevelt.

"He gave me this for my tenth birthday. Look there, he wrote on it: 'For Johnny, with love.' "

J.P. shook his head and replaced the photograph reverentially upon his desk. "Yes, he was a great man — and it's time for the truth. For a sweeping-away of myths. The first Berenson biography will have an automatic sale. You'll make a lot of money. I'll provide that material — about my father, and myself. My own life has been — not without interest. And I'd like it known that there's nothing sinister about my privacy. That Avonhurst is not the fulcrum of the CIA! I'll be fifty-five years old in November, Dave. It's time for a change of image."

I just went on staring at the photograph. I felt completely numb.

"Think about it, anyway. At least you know that I understand and sympathize — with you, and your problems. And I want you on my side."

Amazing, I thought. He has slept with my wife and killed my friend, and he wants me on his side.

At that moment, Carol entered the study. She walked towards us and stopped in the middle of the room.

J.P. placed both hands on the desk, bracing himself for whatever axe might fall. I could see now that his shirt was soaked with sweat. When he looked at his daughter, I thought I had never seen such hope and fear mixed into one expression —

After what seemed like an age, she spoke:

"Is he dead?" asked Carol. Her voice was hardly above a whisper.

Berenson could not reply at first. He sank down onto the chair behind his desk; it was as if his legs would no longer support him. He put his face in his hands and sat there, trembling. At last, he replied:

"Yes. He is dead."

Carol nodded. She regarded us both, dispassionately. Her ravaged face showed no emotion. Then she turned on her heel and walked out of the study.

Berenson dropped his head onto his arms and sobbed with relief.

It had taken a year, but he had done it. He had redeemed his pledge. He had cured her.

48

At ten A.M. the first reporters were at the gatehouse. By monitoring police radio bands they had picked up news of the Avonhurst break-in, and of the duffel bag assault. The name of Steve Rice had not yet been connected with the assault, and would not be until the autopsy report was released later that day — so the full media hysteria was still to come.

When the black-and-white squad car returned from the Coroner's Office downtown, it had to inch its way past a line of press cars, all awaiting their turn to enter the estate. Highway patrolmen were controlling the line and keeping the Sunday-morning traffic moving along Benedict Canyon Drive. As the squad car turned left through the gatehouse, security men peered in at the passengers — the lieutenant, next to the driver; Howard and Joey, pale and silent, in the back.

I sat on the terrace with Kathy, watching the party props dismantled all around. The buffet tent subsided like a great red moth between the pool and the pine forest; soundmen unhooked speakers; caterers removed bars and glasses and bottles; electricians detached colored lights from the high branches of trees.

The press had been admitted to Avonhurst for the second time in twenty-five years. Newspaper and TV journalists came and went respectfully, while an ordered line of photographers marched off to record the cut fence, the ransacked pavilion and the slaughtered dogs. No interviews were being given, and the media was not allowed indoors. Guards stood by every entrance to the castle.

I sat with Kathy while all this went on. I had found her in our room when I went back after my talk with J.P. She was lying on the made-up bed, still wearing her red dress. We went out into the sunshine because neither of us could stand being in the room. We did not speak much — there did not seem to be much to say, although it was a comfort to be sitting with her. I am not exactly sure, but I think she even held my hand for a while. We had both known for so long that it was over, and now the actual ending had the feel of an anticlimax. I knew she hated to hurt me, and that in one sense she would always love me; also that there was nothing in the world that I could ever do to get her back again. I wanted to weep, but no tears came from that emptiness — only the knowledge that what had died could never be replaced; that a great piece of my life had fallen into the ocean.

We sat watching as Howard and Joey came through the bougainvillea-covered archway. Howard's arms overflowed with several pounds' weight of Sunday newspapers. I made out one headline: MALE MODEL KILLED IN BEL AIR. Howard carried the papers over to the pool and laid them carefully around a chaise longue. I supposed he was about to go through them for reports of last night's celebration. The musical event of the year. But after spreading them all out he just sat there staring at the workmen, who were dismantling the plank stage upon which Steve had first met Stephanie.

Joey stood in the middle of the lawn, hand-held camera on his shoulder, wondering what to film first. He saw us sitting together on the terrace and waved. It was a very subdued wave.

At two P.M. the corridor outside the autopsy room on the first floor of the Hall of Justice was full of journalists and TV cameramen, waiting for the coroner's announcement — and for the identity of the duffel bag victim. When Steve's magic name was spoken there was an awed hush, followed by a panic of activity. Even by Los Angeles standards, this was news.

The coroner's report made grim reading. The boys had been thorough — it was as though Steve's physical beauty had in some profound sense offended them. A knife had been slid into each of his nostrils, and the perfect nose ripped from his face; his throat had been slashed, and the vocal cords which had given such joy to millions were laid bare like the strings of an old guitar; the famous blond hair had been hacked from his head and used to staunch the worst of the bleeding; and even the coroner's assistant was surprised to discover, upon forcing open the mouth, that Steve's penis had been lodged in his throat. (A mutilation rarely seen since 1943, when it was regularly employed by Yugoslavian partisans against the occupying German troops.)

49

ROCK STAR SLAIN STOP STEVE RICE BATTERED TO
DEATH AT MULTIMILLIONAIRE'S ESTATE STOP DUFFEL BAG
KILLING FOLLOWS AVONHURST BREAK-IN STOP J.P. BERENSON
LOSES FORTUNE IN JADE STOP LOOKALIKE MODEL STEPHANIE
TIED-UP BUT UNHARMED STOP

The media barrage began on Monday morning. TV pro-
grams were interrupted for the latest information. Car radios
spoke of little else. Much was made of the killers' macabre
choice of target — the home of previous victim Carol Berenson. Their diseased minds were underscored by the Biblical
quotes ("Lead us not into temptation," "Forgive us our trespasses") and — not for the first time in California — paranoia
bred itself and the shock waves turned to fear. The murderous weekend had shaken everyone. Until now the "duffel bag
gang" had been regarded as a danger to late-night hitchhikers
and hustlers — people who were, in a sense, asking for it. But
now they had planned and executed a perfect break-in at one
of the most heavily guarded properties in Bel Air — so it
followed that no one was safe. The sale of firearms at one
Beverly Hills sporting-goods store tripled overnight. The
price of guard dogs rocketed, despite gruesome photographs
of the cavalier manner in which they had been treated at
Avonhurst; private security forces increased their personnel,
and locksmiths reported an unprecedented demand.

The police department took a tremendous hammering. It
was the fourth duffel bag assault in a year, without even the

suggestion of an arrest. Several newspapers called for the resignation of Superintendent Kellerman.

In this atmosphere of tension, Huey Stander was accorded a police escort to Los Angeles International Airport. He wore his Pierre Cardin summer suit, and was accompanied by Floyd, Jason and Jay — all carrying Adidas tennis bags. As a top Berenson aide, Huey was mobbed by reporters on arrival. He told them it was not surprising that, out of two hundred guests, no one had seen or heard anything unusual — the Japanese pavilion was situated some ten minutes' walk from the lawn on which the party had taken place. Mister Berenson was totally distraught, as they could imagine. The theft of the jade meant little to him, but he blamed himself for Steve Rice's death — in that his security arrangements had proven inadequate. At the same time he realized that the break-in had been a great job, from someone who really understood electronics. Fortunately his daughter had slept through the whole commotion. Huey doubted if, even today, Carol knew that her original attackers had been so close. The real tragedy was that Steve had wandered off like that and gotten himself into the path of those maniacs. Huey doubted whether they had even been aware of who they were killing.

Floyd added that Steve's death was a real blow for young people everywhere. Steve was a real hero, they were honored to have met him and to have been among the last folks to talk with him. Jay summed up by saying that Steve Rice would never die. He would live forever through his music — on which optimistic note they all marched off to Huey's executive jet.

At the same time, in a ranch house near Death Valley and the state line, two hundred miles northeast of Los Angeles, the hook-nosed man lowered a newspaper and shouted through an open doorway: "Hey! Some fucker's killed Steve Rice!"

The thin-faced driver appeared in the doorway; he had grown a moustache since the assault on Carol a year before, but apart from that he looked the same. He still wore the turquoise ring and the wide, metal-edged belt.

The hook-nosed man threw down the newspaper. "They say we did it."

The driver picked up the newspaper and began to read. In the room beyond, a woman stirred food in a pot.

The hook-nosed man stood up and crossed to the window. He stared out at the desolate, rock-strewn desert landscape. Beyond a clump of sagebrush stood the Toyota truck, and two fairly new-looking dune buggies. He turned back into the room. The decomposing stone walls were covered with posters, mostly *Playboy* nudes, mixed with music stars: Jimi Hendrix, Janis Joplin, Brian Jones.

The driver lit a cigarette with a gold Dunhill lighter. "Whoever did it got two million dollars' worth of jade," he said.

"He was my favorite." The hook-nosed man seemed genuinely distressed. "I slept out all night one time just to see him."

"Take it easy," said the driver.

"I bought all his records."

"You stole most of them. Look — he was staying at that girl's house!"

"What girl?"

The driver went on reading.

"I only learned the guitar because of him." The hook-nosed man crossed to a battery-operated hi-fi unit in the corner of the room. He selected a tape, pressed a switch and sat down on the floor, chin upon clenched fists. Steve's passionate voice rose on the desert air. "Who would want to kill him?"

"The funeral's Wednesday," said the driver.

On the porch outside the ranch house, the spectacled man was sitting in the sun. He wore cut-off jeans and a straw sombrero. There was a shotgun beside him. When he heard the music, he lowered his comic book and smiled.

Lying in his open coffin, Steve was a triumph of the embalmer's art: hands folded across embroidered voile shirt, an expression of peaceful resignation on his reconstructed face. He looked small, ageless and inhuman. The funeral began with a private service at Howard Vance's Brentwood mansion. Joey filmed the whole thing. Against a taped background of Mozart's Requiem, the priest read a passage from the Gospel according to Saint John, and then a stanza from T.S. Eliot (" . . . spirit of the river, spirit of the sea,/Suffer me not to be separated/And let my cry come unto Thee.").

There were about a hundred mourners, including the backup group and their wives, all the members of our tour entourage, and fifty or so of the most important music names from the Avonhurst party. When the Mozart ended, I thought for a moment that the black superstar was going to sing, but she was apparently too moved. Susie and Kate sobbed noisily throughout and Kellerman kept glaring at them, but apart from that the service passed off without incident.

I looked once at Kathy. She was standing beside J.P., with her head bowed and her hands clenched; I could not guess what she was thinking. Carol Berenson stood nearby. She was dressed in black, and her expression was inscrutable. She never took her eyes away from Steve's corpse, and when the priest intoned "Amen" she echoed it faintly, a beat or two after everyone else — thereby attracting many sympathetic glances. (Was that rehearsed? Her cure had been kept secret, of course, and I later learned that she had attended the funeral only in the teeth of J.P.'s displeasure: he was totally opposed to any public appearance at that time.)

After the service the photographers took flash shots of Stephanie leaning over the coffin for her final farewell. She looked exactly like Steve again — even down to the voile shirt.

The press were delighted with the effect. ("Like she was staring at a mirror.") For an awful moment I thought she was going to kiss Steve goodbye, but fortunately she did not. It would have been a cosmetic disaster.

There was only one outsider — Steve's father — who had flown in from London the day before and now stood, jet-lagged and confused, beside Howard. He could not bring himself to look at his son, and he seemed completely bewildered by the ceremony. Mr. Rice had never understood either Steve or his music, but they had genuinely liked each other, and his grief was true. His wife had died while Steve was still at school, so the father had assumed both parental roles — worrying about his boy's late hours, refusing to go to bed until after he had come home, pacing the gloomy streets of Brixton at night, anxiously visualizing God-knew-what dissipations in the jazz clubs of southeast London. When Steve earned his first money and moved west to Richmond, Mr. Rice felt hurt and rejected, but he did his best not to show it. Steve told me once of his father's last advice to him upon leaving home: "When you drink a pint of beer in hot weather," counselled Mr. Rice, "always look down into the glass because there might be a wasp in there." Steve never forgot that. Now the old man stood surrounded by strangers far from Brixton — and confronted by a painted and perfumed cadaver from which he would shortly inherit a fortune. You could tell that he felt no joy in it.

By the time the photographers had finished with Stephanie, there were about forty thousand fans in the streets around Howard's mansion. Two thousand had slept there overnight, in trucks or cars or camping on grass verges, private driveways, even the roads themselves. By noon all traffic had been diverted from the area, and National Guardsmen were helping police and sheriff's deputies to control the crowd. Helicopters hovered overhead in the dull, smoggy sky; the heat had broken the day before.

At a signal from Kellerman the gates of the mansion were opened and the fans were allowed a final glimpse of their hero. For the next three hours an estimated twenty thousand shuffled to the end of Howard's entrance hall, past the roped-off coffin, and then out again. Invited mourners watched this procession from the steps of a wide staircase. Joey filmed it from there too.

There were some familiar faces in the file-past: the Delaneys, for instance. (Kellerman was the only one to recognize them.) The Delaneys had always felt personally involved in these duffel bag attacks, and had been shocked by the latest tragedy at the home of the very girl they had failed to stop for one year before. They felt responsible for Carol's condition, and had written on four occasions to J.P., each time protesting their sorrow and regret. However, the mountains of sympathetic mail had been handled by the offices of Berenson International, and the Delaneys' expiatory notes elicited no more than stencilled thank-you replies. Nevertheless, when Mrs. Delaney reached the end of the hallway, she looked eagerly from left to right, hoping to catch at least a glimpse of the slender blonde who had raised brown arms to them that night on Coldwater Canyon. She left disappointed, never dreaming that she had stared straight at Carol — who sat beside Joey on the seventh step of the staircase.

Over the next hour, I saw the girl who had grabbed Steve on our first morning in L.A.; also the teenaged waitress who had almost exchanged her honor for his autograph. I saw two paraplegics from Denver (still in their wheelchairs) and many, many faces from our tour; faces that had pressed against car windows, or waited for hours in the rain outside hotels; faces contorted by joy at airport barriers, delirious in the dark auditoriums of concert halls.

When the spectacled man reached the front of the long line, of course, I did not know him at all. He drew abreast of the coffin and paused for a moment, gazing down at Steve.

His owl-face was sad and solemn. Then he looked up and rubbed his head in a puzzled manner, smiling that curious smile of his —

Which was how Carol Berenson happened to recognize him.

50

After the funeral I moved into an apartment building owned by Berenson International on Sunset Strip. Kathy remained at Avonhurst.

For the first three days I did little else but sleep. Food appeared regularly, cooked and served by a silent Mexican girl who inhabited the maid's room. The apartment was Los Angeles modern: glass-topped tables, white rugs, potted plants, Peruvian sculpture. The rear windows looked south, and on a clear day you could see right across the Santa Monica Freeway past Culver City to the airport. From the front you could hear the faint rumble of traffic along the Strip. There was an excellent stereo system, and a large selection of records. The air conditioning worked, and — by peering out of the bedroom window — you could see exactly who was at the pool and decide whether or not you wanted to go down and join them.

Kathy telephoned every day to find out how I was. I dreaded these calls because I was very much afraid of making an idiot of myself, but she was so kind and matter-of-fact that mostly I could pick up the tone from her. On the few occasions when I could not, she simply talked right through my silences and nine times out of ten I was able to muster some sort of rational closing remark. I suppose I felt that any relationship with Kathy was better than none, and since I was now cast in the role of confidant, I might as well accept it. Her only real news was that Berenson was taking her to Japan at the end of the month, with Carol.

There was one breezy phone call from Huey, who was back in town on some unexpected business, and was staying at the Beverly Hills Hotel. He suggested that I might call him there if I ever felt like a game of tennis. Any day around six would be good. Howard Vance's secretary also called regularly, and by the end of the week invitations were beginning to arrive for dinner parties at the homes of well-known names in the music and film worlds. My stock with the answering service rose daily. Copies of my TV plays were flown to Los Angeles with unprecedented speed, and a complimentary paragraph about me appeared in *Variety*; Howard Vance mentioned my name on a talk show, and there was an inquiry from an executive at Columbia regarding my availability to collaborate on a movie about rock music; an important agent took me to lunch at The Bistro, where he introduced me to several girls of startling beauty, and also expressed his desire to represent me on the Coast; an account was opened in my name at the Beverly-Wilshire branch of the Bank of America, and when the chequebook and documents arrived, I saw that the initial deposit had been classified as "L.A. expenses." I began to understand how Berenson senior built the empire.

And through it all I followed the daily press and TV coverage of the veterans' arrest:

After recognizing the spectacled man, Carol had behaved with remarkable coolness — rising from her position on the stairs and walking down to where Berenson stood talking to Kathy and Steve's father. She turned J.P. aside and pointed to the man, who was by then awaiting his turn to leave. By the time he had reached the laurel-lined street outside Howard's mansion, he was being tailed by the lieutenant and three of Kellerman's best detectives. He had parked the Toyota truck several blocks away and — in the crush of mourning fans — the policemen almost lost him twice, locating him the second time only because of the truck, which fitted exactly with the Salinas-girl's description. In the congestion of traffic it took them all half an hour to get clear of the area and, by the time the Toyota had reached the San Diego Freeway and turned north, it was heading an entire convoy of camouflaged police cars.

The spectacled man turned out to be a simple creature. He never once realized that he was being followed, and it had never occurred to him that he ran any risk by attending Steve Rice's funeral. A deeply religious man, he had been released from Camarillo — a state mental hospital — two years before, and for the greater part of his stay there he had believed himself to be John the Baptist. Apart from one stop for gasoline and another for coffee, he led the police straight to Death Valley. After that, an LAPD helicopter took over, shadowing him from on high across the dusty wasteland. One hour later Kellerman himself flew in and took charge of a massive raid on the ranch house. The three suspects — surprised while eating their dinner — offered no resistance.

During their initial search, the detectives found a large store of food, gasoline and medical supplies; two stolen dune buggies; several thousand dollars' worth of stolen stereo equipment; a pile of Vietnam-issue duffel bags; Carol Berenson's gold lighter and black fountain pen. (The Cartier watch had evidently been sold.)

Two days later a second search proved even more fruitful — as I expected it might. In a dry gully some fifty yards east of the ranch house, detectives came upon a large plastic bag of the type normally used for garbage. This bag had been carefully concealed underneath earth and sagebrush and was found to contain the two million dollars' worth of jade taken from Avonhurst, three M-16 Vietnam-issue rifles, various stolen credit cards and a pair of wire cutters. When the Scientific Investigation Division of LAPD identified these wire cutters as having been used during the Berenson break-in, the circumstantial case against the veterans was complete.

The fact that they passionately denied all knowledge of the

plastic bag carried little weight. Their credibility was low. They had freely confessed, twenty-four hours after arrest, to the attacks on Carol Berenson and on a girl in Salinas the year before. The driver (who was the brother of the spectacled man) had a prison record for assault, auto theft and the use of stolen credit cards. The hook-nosed man had spent several months at Inyo County Jail in Independence, California, charged with the theft of electronic equipment. As U.S. Army conscripts, both had been involved in search-and-destroy missions in the Song May region of South Vietnam in 1968. The driver had been a vehicle mechanic, the hook-nosed man a radio operator: he was considered to possess at least enough electrical knowledge to have short-circuited the Avonhurst fence.

During the week they were positively identified by the girl from Salinas, the *L.A. Times* delivery boy (who said he saw them leaving Hillcrest Drive) and Stephanie. The fact that the driver's moustache had never been mentioned before was regarded as unimportant: the delivery boy had only glimpsed them, while Stephanie had only seen them among the moon shadows of the clearing at Avonhurst. The absence of fingerprints on the contents of the plastic bag was also thought irrelevant: as Kellerman had remarked after Carol's assault, these men were careful that way.

Nevertheless, Berenson had been lucky. The last thing he could have foreseen was that his shock cure would flush out the real assailants of his daughter, and thereby subject him to the direct charge of a copycat killing. However, the veterans were not able to prove they had been anywhere else Friday and Saturday, and their denial of the Hillcrest and Avonhurst attacks was put down to the capital nature of these offenses. Also, the copycat charge was fairly incredible: what possible motive could Berenson (or anyone, for that matter) have for murdering — on successive nights — a gay hustler and a world-famous singer?

Still, it did occur to me to wonder whether J.P. would ever allow them to come to trial. There would be publicity, and I should have thought that a burst of gunfire in the desert would have been far simpler. After their arrest I kept expecting to read that they had been murdered in their cells by frenzied Steve Rice fans, or whatever. I imagine that, had the veterans' case been stronger, something of the sort would have happened. I am sure that J.P. must have weighed up all these possibilities with his usual precision and then, for whatever reason, decided to let the law take its course — restricting himself only to helping it along a little. (Thus, while the prosecution was handled by one of the most brilliant lawyers in California, the defense attorney was a family man of retirement age, unlikely to be looking for trouble.)

The day after the truckers were committed for trial, I received a telephone call from Stephanie. She had been reading about me in the trade press, and wondered if we might meet. She was becoming quite a celebrity in her own right now, her delicate features merging with Steve's on *Reflections* billboards across the city.

It turned out that, although she had only seen me once — during the magical Avonhurst meeting — my presence there, at the high point of her life, gave me a special value in her eyes. Also, she took me for Steve's best friend — which for all I know I might have been (God help him). Since his death their encounter had acquired the force of a myth for Stephanie: she now believed she had lost the first and only love of her live — and it was a relief to have someone other than the press to talk to about it.

We went to a quiet restaurant on Melrose Avenue, where the food was very good. During dinner she told me of all they said and did to each other in the clearing before the Japanese pavilion. She was still baffled by whatever it was that Steve had been trying to remember — by whatever memory had so jolted him before the three killers appeared. As a remark,

"So that's who she was" meant nothing to Stephanie, and of course I could not risk enlightening her. It is possible that she will wonder about that for the rest of her days. Then, after all the talk and the wine, the evening came to a traditional but welcome conclusion in my apartment. (Which is how I was able to describe her earlier lovemaking with some conviction. If only all literary research could be that enjoyable.)

At last, about a week before he was due to leave for Japan, J.P. Berenson paid me a visit. He arrived in good spirits, carrying a boxful of confessional tapes recorded by the truckers while in prison. I opened a bottle of California Chablis, and we sat drinking as flat, toneless voices told of Carol's ordeal, from the moment she jumped out in front of the Toyota to the time she was thrown, hog-tied and crippled, back onto Coldwater Canyon Drive. Each man, interrogated separately, accused the others, and after some time a coherent picture emerged from which I was able to construct the opening chapters of this book. The most recent tape featured the hook-nosed man's emotional account of the day he first learned of Steve Rice's death. (This one-and-only display of feelings was subsequently described by the prosecution as a very poor attempt at acting.)

After that, J.P. recounted the horrors of the Cedars-Sinai Medical Center, and of his conversations with Kellerman, Howard and the neurologist. He told me about the months of waiting and hoping and watching from hallways as Carol stood, draped in her silver scarf, before the mirrors of Avonhurst. More importantly, he told me of his vow — his solemn, sacred vow — to cure her at whatever cost.

He told me all this, and more, He talked for an hour. He pieced together the whole story for me. He seemed determined that there should be nothing I did not know, appreciate and (therefore) condone. He faltered only towards the end, while relating Carol's version of the night she hijacked Steve: how she had waited half drunk among the oleanders beneath that bathroom window, before driving them through the hot night to her secret place in Coldwater Canyon. She made no excuses. She had analyzed her behavior with a merciless honesty which alarmed her father. She even said that Steve had been right to desert her. Carol's self-contempt was now the only shadow across J.P.'s happiness — that, and the fragile quality of her voice. For the voice had no power to it, no volume. She murmured and sighed and whispered; you had to lean close to make out what she was saying. She was unable to raise the pitch of it, even though exhaustive tests had revealed no fault. The problem was psychological — some residual inhibition rooted in a fear which they all hoped would pass. Maybe on the trip to Japan.

The sun had set while he talked — the lights were coming on all over Los Angeles. I walked to the window and stared out at the beauty of that man-made landscape: a sea of neon-violet signs, mingling with the dying red of the sunset.

His honesty had impressed me — even though his motives were transparent: he was falling more and more in love with Kathy, and he knew how much I still meant to her. He believed, with some reason, that to know all was to forgive all. My opinion mattered because of my wife, it was as simple as that. The truth was the price he was paying me for her.

I had only one objection: could he still pretend that Steve's death was an accident? After the coroner's report? He knew nothing of the mutilations, he said. He had been occupied with Carol. But it was unforgivable. They were wild dogs, those boys. He had ordered Huey to stop them, but it had been too late. He agreed that the death was (indirectly) his fault. He had been preoccupied with his daughter. He regretted this, but still insisted that it had been an accident. As for the mutilations, well, he supposed, since Steve was already dead . . .

And the Hillcrest killing? He knew nothing of that. That was Huey's affair. Huey had considered it necessary, although of course there should have been no death, merely a beating-up: a prelude to the shock cure. But they were animals, those boys. They were the Furies. Huey could not control them. They would not be used again. Who could trust such degenerates? They were sick.

On that note he stood up and shook my hand. I accompanied him to the elevator, and saw Ace waiting in the corridor. He had been waiting out there the whole time.

I returned to the apartment, locked the door and sat for a long time, gazing at the skyline. So there it was — the whole story, or anyway all I would ever know of it. I could write it down, if I chose. I would have to improvise here and there, invent some dialogue to give coherence to the narrative. But I knew it all now, and I felt more impotent than ever. What could I do? Certainly nothing for Steve, nor for that unfortunate male hustler, come to think of it. I brooded awhile on power; on the nature of power. I recalled those other two writers who had — through courage and perseverance — recently exposed an even greater cover-up, finally dethroning the president of the United States. Well, I thought, it had been their country; there had been two of them, with the power of a great newspaper behind them. I was alone, and I had nothing. I am not Robert Redford. There was nothing I could do.

The music world had accepted Steve's death with its usual passivity. Most of them, on first hearing the news, presumed an overdose. No one had expected him to live long anyway. So many rock stars died young, and violently — their wounds psychic or self-inflicted. He had already completed his best work, and had been actively destroying himself ever since the *Self-Made Man* album. It was almost as if the duffel bag gang had saved him the trouble. And of course, as Jay had remarked, he would live forever through his music.

The veterans' trial would be brief. They would be convicted, sentenced to life imprisonment, and eligible for parole after ten years (which was about what they deserved, in my opinion).

Stephanie was in constant demand — photographed daily awash with romantic despair. All the major studios wanted her, and the surprise was that she seemed to have talent as well.

Kellerman was the local hero. After personally arresting the truckers at the height of their notoriety, his career and reputation were secured. An honorable retirement stretched ahead of him.

Howard had nothing to complain of either. *Reflections* looked set to become one of the highest-grossing LPs of all time, and his *Steve Rice in L.A.* movie had now acquired an almost religious significance. The rush was on to edit Joey's Avonhurst (Spanish chapel) footage and cut it together with his films of the tour and the funeral — the whole package to be released with the album. Howard was frequently seen around town with the Kellerman girls, together and separately, and had been at last relieved of his duty visits to Avonhurst: since Carol was cured she had expressed no desire to see him.

Since Carol was cured.

This has been the story of Carol Berenson, and it was Kathy who completed it for me.

51

She sat alone in her high-school bedroom, gazing at a copy of the *Los Angeles Times*. The headline read THREE DEAD IN BERENSON PLANE CRASH.

> All three passengers died when an executive jet owned by Berenson International crashed yesterday shortly after takeoff from New York's La Guardia Airport. Eyewitnesses reported an explosion toward the rear of the jet, moments after it cleared the runway. Passengers were identified as Floyd Stander, nephew of top Berenson aide Huey Stander, Jason Joyce and his brother Jay Joyce. The pilot, who survived with second-degree burns, is currently hospitalized in the Bronx.

Beneath the article were photographs of Floyd, Jason and Jay. They were all smiling happily at the camera. Carol propped the newspaper on the dressing table and studied these photographs for some time.

Eventually she stood up and opened her closet. She took out the silver scarf and tied it around her shoulders, then stared back at herself in the mirror. Her appearance had been transformed. Her hair was cut into a deep fringe, and sculpted around her cheeks and neck. Some gray remained, but now it resembled fashionable streaks. She wore dark glasses and a summer suit from Yves St. Laurent. She returned to the dressing table, took a sealed envelope from her pocket and placed it beside the newspaper. The envelope bore just one word: *Daddy.*

She walked to the door and picked up her crocodile bag. She stood for a moment, looking around at the memorabilia on the walls. Then she walked out.

Berenson was lying on a chaise longue by the pool. A huge umbrella cast a circle of shade across him. The pool glittered angrily in the afternoon sun. Kathy lay beside him.

Carol came down the steps of the south terrace and saw them lying together beside the pool. She paused. There was the sound of bees buzzing amongst the rosebushes. A hummingbird hovered above the Giacometti statue, then drifted away.

Kathy sensed a presence. She looked across and saw Carol. She said something to J.P., who sat up immediately and turned.

Carol walked off towards the bougainvillea-covered archway.

In the courtyard, her yellow Ferrari shimmered in the heat. The top was down and Carol threw her bag into the back. She opened the door, slid into the driver's seat and twisted the ignition key. The engine fired and she pushed the selector lever forwards just as her father walked through the archway. Kathy appeared behind him. Carol waved to them, shifted her foot to the accelerator, and drove away.

J.P. waved back and watched her out of sight around the double twist of the drive. His face showed no emotion. Ace came into the courtyard, and J.P. nodded. Ace climbed into the Jaguar.

Kathy protested: "You're not having her followed, are you? Your own daughter?"

Berenson ignored this. He walked up the front steps and into the castle. Half an hour later he went into Carol's room and found the letter:

Dear Daddy,
   I cannot go to Japan with you, or anyplace. My only chance

[227]

now is to live apart from you. I guess this will hurt, but I have had nothing else to do for a year but think, and I know I am right. I know the terrible thing you have done, and I know you did it for me, as always. You gave me everything all my life at whatever cost and I always took it as if it were my right. You taught me to take whatever I wanted, that was our code and we lived by that. Only this time the price was too high. Well, now there is nothing left of Carol, the spoiled bitch you created. I think she died that night in the canyon. I can speak again now, but I have nothing left to say. I don't know what is left. Maybe there is someplace I can find out. Well, there are a hundred ways you can find me and bring me back, even though I am nineteen now and can spend Grandfather's money. But I hope you will not. You know I will never speak of what has happened and I ask only to be left alone to start my life over. Do that for me, Daddy. I pray that you will and you will be happy. I still love you.

Caro

J.P. sat on her narrow bed for a long time. His head was bowed. He read the letter again and again — those blue pages with their round, childish handwriting and their desperate sentiments. He knew that he had lost her.

Ace reported back two hours later. He had tailed Carol to Los Angeles International Airport, where she had caught the TWA afternoon flight to Paris, France. She had left her Ferrari in the airport garage. Ace had not realized until the last moment that she would board the airplane — up to then he had presumed that, without luggage, she was meeting someone there. But nothing could be simpler than to call Paris and have her stopped at Charles de Gaulle —

Nothing could be simpler, but they did not do it. J.P. understood that — for now at least — he must let her go. Whether he also realized that she was right to go, I do not know. Kathy says he did.

For myself, I escaped to London as soon as possible — far

from Avonhurst and its savage lord. As I write these lines I am back in Fulham, and the rain is coming down. I have had many months of learning to live without Kathy, but I am still not very good at it. There are still the solitary Sunday walks (true test of emotional status). There is still the regular arrival of despair. But I am not entirely unhappy: for in the end I found the courage to refuse Berenson's offer.

I have recently learned that J.P. had more than one reason for offering me the biography. I had assumed it to be a payoff, an acceptable way of handing me a large cheque — but it now turns out that a former *New York Times* journalist, after many years of Berenson-watching, is preparing a highly critical account of J.P.'s father, and especially of his activities during World War Two. So my function was to get in first with J.P.'s version: thereby adding one more shabby item to the catalogue of compromise which has been my career — betrayal of my early promise. But in the end I could not do it. Two other biographers are now at work — there is no shortage of writers. But I doubt that either of them will ever know the joy I felt upon returning the Berenson cheque, and then using his material to construct this narrative. (And to be honest at last — for only here, in this book, free from deadlines and pressures, have I finally told the truth. Could redemption be at hand?)

Well, either way I have set the record straight. Whether anyone believes it, or even reads it, is another matter. It is all here. It is written down. It seemed the least I could do — for Steve, and for Carol —

For Carol, with her bright belief in her inherent right to the best things of the world; and for Steve, who fell into that category for her — along with Ferraris and crocodile bags. He was a status symbol, he was the tops. She took a certain amount of trouble to get him and then — when he did not work out — she was disappointed.

Now Carol has paid for all that. I hope she will be happy.

According to Kathy, she has settled in France. She has bought a converted farmhouse in deep countryside near Aix-en-Provence, not far from a Carmelite convent to which she is rumored to have donated a large sum. She lives alone, protected by an army of servants, several of whom spy for her father. But, although he has her watched, he does so unobtrusively. He never contacts her directly. He plays a waiting game. Until now she has not asked to see him, and I do not know whether she ever will. For J.P. Berenson, atonement could last a lifetime. Meanwhile, the media have given her up. They have dubbed her The Silent Heiress, and written her off. People are beginning to forget.

Even for me, absorbed as I am with rebuilding my own life, the episode fades a little more each day. Except for one last image which haunts me still.

On the morning I left Los Angeles, Ace drove me to the airport. He had time on his hands — Berenson was already in Japan with Kathy — and we used the bulletproof Cadillac, the one built for Guggenheim in 1938. I was pleased about that, it seemed the right way to go. I sat in the front and gazed up at the high billboards, many of which reflected Steve and Stephanie — their overlapping profiles mirroring each other against the azure sky. Every band on the car radio seemed to be playing tracks from the newly released *Reflections* album, so I left as I arrived — to the music of Steve Rice.

Ace was in a talkative mood, especially on the subject of Carol Berenson, whom he had never liked. However, he admired her recent behavior and (although the least impressionable of men) he had been unexpectedly moved by a detour she made in her yellow Ferrari the afternoon she left Avonhurst. Ace had tailed her at a discreet distance — he was good at that — north for a few miles, east along Mulholland, and then south. He assumed she was just driving around when, without warning, she disappeared down a narrow lane off Coldwater Canyon Drive. He accelerated and reached the top of the lane in time to see her car bump out of sight. Ace parked beside the turnoff, lowered the window, and inhaled the still, scented air. He was considering what to do, when a truck appeared — chugging uphill towards the Valley. As he watched the truck out of sight, Ace all at once remembered that this could be the very stretch of road (well known from newspaper reports) onto which Carol's hog-tied body had been thrown the year before.

He stepped out of the car and closed it carefully. He felt under his arm for the gun he always carried, then picked his way along the narrow lane, through close groves of mingled palms, olives, and eucalyptus. After a hundred yards or so, he stopped.

And stared.

There was the charred and twisted oak tree and there, kneeling beneath it, was Carol. Her face was raised, her eyes were closed, and she was weeping. Everything that grew seemed motionless.

Ace stepped back out of sight.

At that moment, she cried out to the empty sky — a long, sobbing cry. It sounded like "Help me."

And the sound she made was loud and full and clear. Ace said he was surprised at the depth to which this cry echoed through the canyon.